What the critics are saying...

...so well-written that the readers will cheer these two people on while feeling their hurts, their triumphs, and their happiness. You're in for a treat! ~ *Fallen Angels*

...an exciting book from the very beginning. ...so many undercurrents it kept me glued. ...a book I'll read over and over. ~ *Romance Junkies*

"Toe curling, fantasy inducing, and extremely kinky. ...a compelling read. ...set the sheets on fire." ~ *Romance Reviews Today*

Vonna Harper

DANGEROUS RIDE

ELLORA'S CAVE
ROMANTICA PUBLISHING

An Ellora's Cave Romantica Publication

www.ellorascave.com

Dangerous Ride

ISBN #1419952315
ALL RIGHTS RESERVED.
Dangerous Ride Copyright© 2005 Vonna Harper
Edited by: *Sue-Ellen Gower*
Cover art by: *Syneca*

Electronic book Publication: February, 2005
Trade paperback Publication: August, 2005

Warning:

The following material contains graphic sexual content meant for mature readers. *Dangerous Ride* has been rated *E-rotic* by a minimum of three independent reviewers.

Ellora's Cave Publishing offers three levels of Romantica™ reading entertainment: S (S-ensuous), E (E-rotic), and X (X-treme).

S-*ensuous* love scenes are explicit and leave nothing to the imagination.

E-*rotic* love scenes are explicit, leave nothing to the imagination, and are high in volume per the overall word count. In addition, some E-rated titles might contain fantasy material that some readers find objectionable, such as bondage, submission, same sex encounters, forced seductions, etc. E-rated titles are the most graphic titles we carry; it is common, for instance, for an author to use words such as "fucking", "cock", "pussy", etc., within their work of literature.

X-*treme* titles differ from E-rated titles only in plot premise and storyline execution. Unlike E-rated titles, stories designated with the letter X tend to contain controversial subject matter not for the faint of heart.

Dangerous Ride

Chapter One

"How'd you do it? I would have bet the farm that bronc had you."

"Not tonight." Still breathing hard, Maita wiped her sweaty palms on her jeans-clad thighs and tried to lift the thick single braid off the back of her neck. Why hadn't she cut off the mass? "I watched him earlier and knew he'd lead with his left leg. I was ready for him."

"You sure as hell did. And you looked sexy as shit doing it."

Maita Compton had to laugh. She'd only met Ann shortly after coming to Klamath County a couple of weeks ago, but it hadn't taken long to realize the young woman didn't pull her punches.

"I wasn't thinking sexy," Maita admitted from where she and Ann now stood behind the arena where the local rodeo was being held. Clapping and stomping feet from the spectators in the wooden stands briefly made conversation impossible and gave her a few moments in which to get her heart rate back to normal.

She loved bareback bronc riding, fed off the "woman versus animal" battle of strength and wits. True, her obsession with physical battles had left her with her share of bruises, scars, and at least two concussions, but she'd yet to find any high to rival the adrenaline rush, the feeling that, finally, she had control. "The only thing that mattered was ending up alive," she finished once the applause died down.

"So why don't you do barrel racing?" Ann asked. As if making her point, she stretched out her arms and turned in a slow circle designed to show off her bright pink and purple outfit complete with fringed sleeves and matching fringes on her cowgirl hat. "The way you're built, the judges will award you first place, particularly if you pop a button and give them a peek at the merchandise."

"Barrels don't do it for me," Maita said as the arena hands across from where she and Ann stood prepared to yank open a gate for another bronc rider.

"Not enough danger? What's with you and your death wish?"

She didn't have a death wish, nothing close to it. As for why she courted broken bones and worse on the back of a 1200-pound animal—some things were no one else's business.

The gate swung open. For an instant, the big-eared roan stood motionless while its rider ground his legs into the animal's sides, one hand in the air, the other caught in the belly rope. Then the horse bellowed and charged. As it ran, it flung its hind legs into the air, threatening to hit the rider on the back of the head. The cowboy was flung forward, then back as the horse hit the ground on all four legs. Once, twice, three times the bronc turned itself into a lathered pogo stick. On the fourth time, the bronc spun in a half-circle at the same time and sent the rider flying. His flight was short-lived, ending in a belly-first landing. The bronc, looking exceedingly proud of itself, continued to run and buck around the perimeter of the arena while the hapless rider gathered his hands and knees under him and looked around for his hat.

"Score one for another Severn horse," Ann said. "They say you can't teach rodeo stock anything, but I swear, his animals are the best."

"Severn?" Maita repeated, her attention back on Ann. "I've heard the name."

"Shit. You should. His land abuts your...your employer's. I don't know how many acres he has...several thousand. He keeps the rodeo stock near the main complex so unless you've had time to do any exploring you probably haven't seen it."

"Time?" Maita laughed. "In my dreams."

"At least he let you have tonight off. Does *he* know you rodeo?"

Something in Ann's tone changed, but Maita couldn't put her finger on it. Since going to work for the McDermit spread as a horse trainer, she'd been kept so busy she'd barely left it. She'd met Ann at a horse auction, and her boss Rylan McDermit had introduced them, saying Maita needed someone her age and sex to talk to in this testosterone-laden world. Rylan's words had held a teasing, maybe taunting tone. Maita hadn't known why, and Ann's mouth had pinched. The two women hadn't said much beyond comments about the weather, but to her surprise, Ann had all but attached herself to her since they'd spotted each other in the rodeo parking lot earlier that night.

"Yes, Rylan knows," Maita said, her attention divided between Ann and preparations for the next ride. So far she was in first place for the bareback event, but only half of the cowboys had completed their rides. "It factored into why he hired me."

"That and your looks."

"He's been a gentleman."

"Has he?"

"Yes."

"Good." Ann's voice dropped. "But don't turn your back on him."

"I can handle myself."

"I'm sure you can."

To Maita's surprise, Ann ran her fingers over her upper arm as if testing her muscle strength—and maybe more. "Damn, that's hard. You work out?"

"Some." Maita didn't move. The touch, lingering and warm, reminded her of how long it had been since she'd been touched. Making it with women wasn't her style, but she wasn't dead. She understood sexual energy.

"More than some. They'll like that."

"They?"

Ann patted her shoulder then stuck her hands in her back pockets in a gesture that accented her small but firm-looking breasts. "You'll learn soon enough." She sighed, blinked repeatedly then shook her head in what Maita interpreted to be resignation. "Let's just say that damn Rylan chose well. And Severn is going to want in on the action."

* * * * *

Maita had been able to dismiss Ann's strange comment during the bull-riding event, but now the small, well-attended, once-monthly rodeo was over. Spectators were making their way to the dirt and gravel parking lots. Holding her second-place ribbon, Maita waited behind the bucking chutes where Ann had told her to stay while she got some details on the post-celebration.

Celebration? Drinking, flirting, maybe an hour wound around some sweaty cowboy? Thoughts of expending weeks of pent-up sexual energy with a man's cock deep in her kicked up her heart rate and heated points south. How long since she'd had sex? And would she, maybe, connect with someone she trusted and had a modicum of something in common with? Much as she loved and needed to frequently fuck, spreading her legs for the hell of it wasn't in her nature. Besides, in today's world a girl had to have a death wish if she didn't keep certain realities in mind.

What was it Ann had said about Rylan choosing well when he hired her? Hell, it wouldn't be the first time she'd gotten a job because she was easy on the eye, but not once had she kept the job based on her looks. Bottom line, she knew horses a hell of a lot better than she understood human beings. Rylan McDermit had to be at least twenty years older than her which put him close to her father in age, not that she knew anything about the man. As employers went, she'd had worse than Rylan who combined a hands-on approach with trusting those he'd hired to do their jobs. Sure she knew he was a man, fit and proud of it with a certain arrogance she attributed to the state of his checking account. So far he hadn't come close to coming on to her, but she'd sensed something in his manner that was slightly unnerving.

Someone must have brought along a CD player because the speakers the announcer had used earlier now blasted out a country and western song about a truck-driving man and the women he'd left behind. Some of the overhead lighting had been turned off, throwing the rodeo grounds into deep and seductive shadows. Not questioning what she was doing, Maita started toward the large county-owned barn behind the arena. She heard laughter and loud voices, mostly male. They drew her magnet-like to the promise of energy, fun, release.

As she neared the main barn opening leading to the twenty or more stalls, she spotted knots of people just inside the barn. Some were standing while others perched on hay bales. The smell of hay, hops, and sweat spoke to her skin and nerve endings. Damn but she loved this hard-living, hard-playing world!

"I was just coming to get you." Ann thrust an opened beer bottle into her hand. "Last rodeo it was so frickin' cold the celebration was cancelled, but it's rocking tonight."

Rocking only began to describe the impact of music loud enough to rattle one's teeth, bowlegged cowboys in tight, tight jeans wrapped around their beers, an arm wrestling match with one of the hay bales serving as a table, several mongrel dogs roaming around, a big-bellied man wearing coveralls backing a big-hipped woman against a stall wall.

"We're in the minority," Ann announced unnecessarily. "At least five men to every woman. Take your pick."

Her pick? From the way several men stared at her, she'd have to beat off the competition—if she wanted to. She spotted Rylan talking to a younger, larger, taller man but didn't bother going over to him. Tonight she was off the clock. Her red ribbon proclaimed her right to be there. What she did on her own time was her own business. Besides, he'd already said she was the best trainer he'd ever had.

Hell, she could have told him that.

"Congratulations, sweet cheeks. You've got balls, I'll hand you that."

Despite being startled, Maita took care to take her time acknowledging the crack. "You're talking about my ride?" she asked a man who had to be a good foot taller than her and in desperate need of a shave. "I hope you bet on me to finish."

He laughed, the sound on a par with the music. "Hell, by the time I realized it was a broad instead of some snot-nosed kid riding it was too late. You've done that before."

"You think?" She took a swallow. Cold and clean, the beer nevertheless warmed her.

"Bareback's a man's sport," he insisted, swaying a little. "You got lucky."

"In your dreams. I know what I'm doing."

"Maybe. Maybe not." He leaned close and gave her a sample of his alcohol-laden breath. "Tell you what, I'll give you some riding lessons."

"I don't need them."

"This kind of lesson." He grabbed his crotch. "I've got something here you're going to love riding better 'n you did that pony. Come on. Jump on board. Ten seconds with me and you'll be flying."

"You couldn't handle me." Her grip on her beer increased.

"Says who, bitch?"

Although she saw it coming, he'd clamped a paw around her forearm before she could get out of his reach. Using his superior size, he yanked her arm behind her and pushed her against him. His flesh felt soft, but there was so damn much of it. Survival instinct firmly held in check, she forced herself to relax. The hand holding her beer hung at her side.

"Is this how you do it, cowboy?" she taunted. "Can't get a woman to look twice at you so you resort to force?"

"Whatever it takes."

"You're pathetic." She glared up at his blurred face. "Beyond pathetic."

"Bitch!" He leaned over her, forcing her to arch her back and turn her head to the side to avoid his wet lips and probing tongue.

She'd started to aim the bottle at the side of his head when she felt him being wrenched away. Backstepping, she saw someone had wrapped his arm around Wet Lips' neck. From the look on Wet Lips' face, he couldn't breathe.

"Back it down, Ted, now!" the newcomer ordered.

Taking advantage of her opportunity, Maita twisted free. Doing so earned her a wrenched shoulder, but it was worth it. The newcomer hadn't relinquished his neck hold—Ted's face was turning purple.

"Let him go," she insisted. "He's going to pass out."

"Don't tell me I interrupted something you were looking forward to," the newcomer drawled. "You like being manhandled?"

"Not by him."

"But you're not opposed to getting roughed up?"

What was that about? "Let him go," she repeated. Ted's eyes had rolled back. "I'm not looking forward to performing CPR on him, and I don't think you are either."

"Good point." He released Ted and shoved him at some nearby hay.

Several people applauded as Ted landed in a heap. Maita struggled with the desire to do a little batting practice with the bottle, using Ted's head as the ball. "Damn him," she muttered, "thinking he's so damn strong."

"He is. Leastwise he's a lot bigger than you."

"Size doesn't mean shit." Determined to calm her agitation, she swallowed deeply. Again, the cold beer did its work on her nervous system. "I could take him."

Her rescuer laughed, forcing her to admit she'd sounded like a boastful adolescent. What he didn't know was she probably wouldn't still be alive if she hadn't learned how to hold her own.

"Just like you took Blue Boy."

For a moment she didn't know what he was talking about. Then she remembered that was the name of the bronc she'd ridden. "You're observant."

"It's my business."

"Your— Are you Kade Severn?"

"Guilty."

"And you're a stock contractor."

"Among other things."

He'd made no attempt to touch her during their short exchange, and yet her skin felt invaded. Telling herself her reaction was the understandable aftermath of having to deal with Ted of the sloppy lips, she made a show of taking in her surroundings. In truth, little beyond him mattered anymore. Unlike the other celebrants who almost universally wore jeans, he was dressed all in black except for the silver belt buckle. His traditional cowboy shirt, complete with pearl snaps, rode his hard and muscular body like a lover and the snug dark pants made no attempt to hide the family jewels. She wouldn't call him handsome—the word conjured up images of smooth, unscarred flesh and a fashion model body.

Instead, Kade Severn struck her as having been carved out of stone. No attempt had been made to sand away the rough edges. He reminded her of a wild horse complete with long, unkempt hair, wounds both old and new, a rogue look to his eyes, body ready for action. If she didn't approach him slow and cautious, he'd bolt.

Or would he? Maybe, like a stallion staking its claim, he'd mount her.

"Ah," she managed belatedly, "just because I rode Blue Boy doesn't mean he isn't a good bronc. I hope you'll continue to use him."

"I intend to." He took her arm and guided her into the shadows. Next he unceremoniously clamped his hands around her waist and lifted her onto a hay bale, then positioned himself in front of her. Dim, naked light bulbs hanging from the rafters cast him in shadow. "Rylan said you're good. When I saw you intended to ride tonight, I made a point of watching."

"You don't usually?" Her throat felt dry, unlike her crotch.

"No," he said. His deep, strong tone slid like warm water over her skin. "I have a lot of duties during a rodeo, too damn many if truth be known."

The rodeo itself was behind them, and although she imagined he still needed to oversee getting his broncs and bulls back to his spread, he'd decided to spend time with her.

Why not? The night was for hard-pounding music, alcohol, seduction.

"I briefly worked for a stock contractor in Wyoming," she told him. "Then the SPCA shut him down."

"I heard about that." He folded his arms across his too-broad chest and latched his dark gaze on her. "You didn't happen to have anything to do with the whistle being blown, did you?"

She'd been instrumental in building a case against a man determined to put profit before the livestock's welfare, but she wasn't about to tell this man that. After all, he and her former employer were in the same business.

"I left the same week the indictment came," she explained. "I don't know what happened."

"You already had another job lined up?"

She shrugged and made a show of savoring her drink. Someone had switched CDs. Now a female singer was demonstrating her range, the notes long, slow, and rich like old wine. Out of the corner of her eye, she spotted three couples engaged in something between a dance and fucking fully clothed. Damn, she needed to be fucked! To fuck.

"Finding work has never been a problem," she said and finished her beer.

"Because you have sure hands."

"Is that what Rylan told you? He approves of the way I handle his green stock?"

"He does, among other things."

What things, she wanted to ask but didn't. She'd have to be dead from the neck down not to know how her boss studied not just her gentle patience with all but wild horses, but her form and movement. Hell, most men did. She'd known the time would come when she and Rylan would need to define their relationship and had been looking forward to the exploration. But that had been before this black-clad cowboy had walked into her life. The thought of sniffing out the possibilities with not one but two men caused her pussy to heat again. Before she could focus on and enjoy the sensation, Kade took hold of her wrists and turned her hands up so he could study her palms.

"Calluses. Short nails," he observed with his thumbs pressing into her veins. "The hands of a woman who sees them as tools."

"I wouldn't be able to do my job if they were soft."

"And pitting yourself against horses that hate any kind of confinement turns you on, does it?"

His words held layers of meaning. Challenge. She wanted to concentrate on them and yet she didn't care...about anything except his thumbs shutting off the flow of blood.

"I'm good at what I do." Her voice had a rote-like quality. "I know how to channel my strength to where it needs to go. After a while the horses I work with know that."

"I'm sure they do."

He started kneading the insides of her wrists, his thumbs making long, sensual strokes along her flesh. If she hadn't been sitting, she'd be hard-pressed to go on standing. The way he stared at her, bold and confrontational, reminded her of a just-roped stallion.

Was that what he was? A stallion?

If so then she was a mare. A mare in heat.

"We're going to dance," he said and pulled her to her feet.

Chapter Two

"You…haven't you heard of asking?" Despite her surprise, Maita didn't try to pull free.

"I've heard of it. But tonight there's no need."

He'd wrapped his arms around her and pressed her against his chest before she could make sense of what he'd just said. Instead of moving to the middle of the barn where several other couples now gyrated to a slow love song, he spread his legs slightly so hers fit within his stance and began rolling their bodies from side to side. Her long, single-braided hair stroked her back. His grip kept her arms against her side when she would have preferred to lay them on his shoulder. The part of her brain long accustomed to making decisions about her life and body demanded to know what the hell he thought he was doing.

The part ruled by her clit didn't give a damn.

As long as they remained where they were, they were nearly hidden from view. The song, sung by a female vocalist with a throaty voice, had long been a favorite of hers, but with her breasts flattened against Kade's strength, she heard nothing except a low percussion beat. The sound and more slid beneath her skin to quicken her blood flow and breathing rate. Her feet remained in place. In fact, unless she was mistaken, only her hips were in motion. Perhaps she should look up and read his expression, but she'd already learned what she needed to know.

He had an erection. Maybe he became aroused by playing macho man. Maybe women who smelled of sweaty horses and leather turned him on.

Her arms felt leaden. Even if she'd been able to lift them, she wouldn't have tried. Her entire body became heavy, inert almost. Well, not all of her, she acknowledged. Everything from belly button to knees had heated. She felt feverish there, the greatest heat centered around her pussy. Hot and melting, she turned small and weak within his embrace. He guided her swaying movements in tune with the song's echoing rhythm. She heard laughter and loud talking, and yet she didn't.

Most of all there was him. Him everywhere. Commanding.

Working with horses had conditioned her to sizes greater than her own, and she'd stopped feeling small around any living thing—until now. Somehow this near stranger had sucked muscle and self-determination out of her, melted her down until she'd become more him than herself.

Beyond comprehension, she loved feeling like this, loved his arms encasing hers, his legs bracketing hers with his sex insistent between them and her back arched. He turned one way and then the other, taking her with him as surely and confidently as she guided well-trained mounts.

She'd become his animal, his compliant possession.

Before she could face the question, he ran his hands from her shoulders down over her arms, her elbows, biceps. Then he guided her arms behind her. More curious than alarmed, she didn't resist as he crossed one wrist over the other and held them in place against her buttocks with one large, work-conditioned hand.

"What are you doing?" she asked as he widened his stance and brought her legs, her hips even, under his control.

"An experiment."

"Experiment? What kind?"

"One designed to determine how far I can go tonight." As if reinforcing the barely comprehended statement, he pressed his free hand against her right ass cheek.

Quit it! If you think I'm going to let you manhandle me, you're sadly mistaken! She thought the words. She just didn't say them.

"Tell me about yourself."

"What?"

"What do you want out of life, Maita?" he asked. His breath chased hot over her face. "You're damn good at what you do. Rylan told me he's never seen better and from what I observed of your ride, you understand a horse's instinct."

"I'll take that as a compliment." *Free yourself, damn it! Let him know what you think of being treated like a just-roped horse!*

"It's acknowledging one kind of mastery by someone who understands the necessary skills and talents."

He hadn't just thrown out the words, she'd bet a month's pay on it. She just wished she understood what he was getting at.

But with her body under his control and her hot to learn what else he had in mind, how did he expect her to hold up her end of this double-edged conversation?

Maybe he didn't.

"Perhaps you're bored by my observations," he whispered in that silken whiskey tone of his. "Maybe you'd rather just dance."

Maybe.

He stopped probing her ass and transferred his attention to her throat, his fingertips an unsettling mix of fine sandpaper and satin. She lost herself in thoughts of those fingers roping a rogue horse or forcing a massive bull into a corral. Hands with that kind of strength would have no trouble getting a woman to comply with anything he wanted, and yet he exuded rough male sex. He'd never have to force a woman—unless he wanted to.

Was his hold on her about pleasing himself? she wondered. He knew nothing about her, couldn't possibly give a damn about anything except getting in her pants. Tomorrow it'd be another conquest—or maybe he'd go back to his wife.

"Are you married?" she demanded as the languid song ended.

"Do you want me to be?"

"What kind of question is that?" She put all her strength into yanking free. When she stood apart from him and rubbed her wrists, she had no doubt she was free because he'd relinquished control.

"If I had a wife, you could tell me to take it home and be rid of me. But if there's no one in my life, it complicates things."

Things were already more complicated than she felt like handling tonight. "What's the answer?"

"No wife."

His answer carried layers of complication. But before she could so much as ask herself if she wanted to wade through them, another song began. This one pounded the air with energy, with anger even. Smiling with just his mouth, Kade captured her right wrist and pulled her into the center of the barn. She didn't know how many other couples had already claimed the dance space, couldn't guess at the number of mostly men who clapped and whistled as they watched the dancers.

In an oddly disturbing way she knew they were garnering more attention than the other couples. As Kade spun her away from him, then quickly pulled her against him, she realized the onlookers' focus was on her and not her partner. She tried to tell herself it was understandable because she was the newcomer, Kade a fixture at the rodeo scene. Still, she couldn't shake the predatory atmosphere. What was she, a brood mare up for auction?

No matter! Couldn't think about that now, not with Kade spinning her this way and that, letting her out as if she was a wild horse testing its rope, then reeling her in tight and tethered. Her wrist throbbed from the tight hold. Yet, she loved the ceaseless movement, the mix of freedom and capture. Maybe he could sense the flesh under his strong fingers, because before discomfort could slide into pain, he deftly ran her in a circle behind him, and when she moved in front again, he switched to her left wrist.

He barely moved. Instead, she absorbed the song's energy and performed the dance for both of them, sweated and spent herself. She became dizzy. Her legs trembled. Sweat ran down her throat to join the wet heat between her breasts.

She loved being part of voice and instruments, of this masculine world. Most of all she loved dancing for Kade Severn. Being what he wanted.

When she thought she might lose her balance and collapse before him, the song abruptly ended. A heartbeat later, the onlookers started clapping and stomping their feet, applauding her.

Ignoring their audience, Kade yanked her against him in a way that had already become familiar. He guided her arms to her sides and pressed them against her hips in an undeniable command for her to keep them there. Then he pulled a cotton handkerchief out of his back pocket and used it to wipe sweat off her cheeks and throat. Displaying his disdain for her right to her own body, he yanked loose the top snap on her shirt and slid the cotton between her breasts.

Shaking and out of breath, she let him.

"She's had enough for one night."

Distracted by the vaguely familiar voice, Maita struggled to find the source. Her boss stood a few feet away. His expression and stance left no doubt of his displeasure.

"I'll decide when she's had enough," Kade retorted.

What was she? Their dual possession?

Yes. If you let it happen.

* * * * *

Still working at controlling her breathing, Maita wetted a paper towel in the women's restroom and used it to wipe sweat off every inch of exposed flesh. She left the hollow between her breasts until last because she wanted to savor the memory of Kade's hands on that part of her anatomy.

What the hell had the exchange between the two men been about?

And even more important, what was her role? The pluses, minuses, danger?

The bathroom door opened, and Ann walked in. The other woman took in the small facility, then locked the door and leaned against it. "Quite an introduction," she said.

"To what?"

"Sorry, girl, but I'm going to let you figure that out." Ann walked over to the sink and started washing her hands. "What do you know about Klamath County?"

"What's to know? It's ranching country, dry. Thousands of heads of beef cattle are raised here. All those ranchers have horses, some for their own need, others, like Rylan, train and then sell them. Winters are harsh, summers too short. Those who don't make a living off the land have a hard time making it which is why there aren't any good-sized towns."

Ann nodded. "You've learned a lot in the short time you've been here."

"I did my research before I took the job." Although she'd managed to cool down considerably, her washing up had done nothing to quiet the heat between her legs. Her single beer had little to do with her condition. *Score one for your side*, she silently told Kade Severn.

"Did you?" Ann shook her head. "Oh, I'm sure you researched the obvious things such as whether Rylan's operation operated in the black. It does, nicely. I'm talking about the undercurrents."

"Undercurrents?" Her mouth felt dry.

Ann swiped her wet hands on her jeans, glanced at her manicure, and returned her gaze. "You're free and twenty-one so I'm not going to tell you how to live your life. Hell, now I've embraced certain things, you'd never get me to turn my back on. I just want you to realize up-front that you've taken the first step down a road I don't believe you've ever been on before. Most women who go on it do so with their eyes open. But with you, they see you as prey."

Alarm slammed into her. "They?"

"Certain men."

"Like Kade Severn?"

"And your boss."

In what now felt like another lifetime, a monster-man had directed the course of her life and made essential decisions without consulting her. When she'd broken free, she'd vowed she'd never again let anyone rule her. And yet hadn't Kade just— "Why are you telling me this?"

"I'm not sure." Another non-smile touched Ann's lips. "Maybe I'm seeing something in you... Let's just say my opportunities for getting the upper hand are far and few between these days. This is one of those chances. And hell, maybe I want you to leave the field open for me."

"What field? How am I—"

"Just keep your eyes and ears open, Maita. Don't take anything at face value. Enjoy the hell out of what happens but know it's a game of win and lose."

"And if I don't want to play?"

Ann indicated her wrists where the imprint of Kade's fingers remained. "It's too late. The game has begun."

She wasn't shaking, she wasn't! "What happens if I lose?"

"Lose?" Ann closed her eyes. "I don't want to think about it. Maybe..." Her lids fluttered open. "No maybe to it. I've got to be honest with you. You'll be fundamentally changed, lessened."

Reduced? "I don't understand!"

"You will, soon. Enjoy the hell out of every moment you're given of the ride, but never lose sight of something." She wrapped her arms around her middle as if hugging herself.

"What?" Maita demanded when the silence dragged on.

"It'll always be a game for Kade and Rylan. I wish— damn, I wish it was otherwise! But shit, they do what they do to women because they see the female sex as horseflesh, property to turn into valuable, highly trained livestock."

"What? Are they insane!"

"Maybe. To tell you the truth, I don't give a damn."

"You don't?"

Emotion flickered across Ann's features then her earlier passivity returned. "I'd be crazy to love a man who doesn't care about me except from the neck down, wouldn't I?" She paused as if trying to convince herself of what she'd just said. "The way I look at it, if a man's willing to give me the best sex I'll ever have, I'd be fool not to put up with what goes along with being fucked—and fucked."

Had Ann been drinking? She didn't smell alcohol on her breath but couldn't be sure. "I, ah, I appreciate the advice."

"Advice, warning, whatever word fits. Just don't fall in love. It'll destroy you if you do."

Maita's mind was still whirling with questions when Ann yanked her shirt out of her jeans and, showing no hint of embarrassment, unzipped her jeans and tugged then down, exposing a string bikini. She widened her stance and pulled red silken fabric away from her crotch. Maita gaped at the tiny gold ring dangling from Ann's clit.

"A gift from Rylan because I was a good girl—his criteria for a good girl anyway. Unfortunately, Kade hasn't touched me since."

Kade? "He—how did Rylan—"

"He pierced me while I was helpless. Oh, I suppose I could have moved, but by then I'd come so many times I couldn't come again. I didn't give a damn about anything." Ann licked her lips and repositioned her bikini so the ring was covered. "The only way I can get it off is by cutting it, and I'm afraid of displeasing—"

"You let Rylan—"

"*Let* isn't part of things where those two men are concerned." Ann started stroking herself through the red fabric. "I know you don't understand yet, but you will. You will."

Before Maita could begin to gather her thoughts, someone knocked on the bathroom door. "Ann." The voice was unmistakably Rylan's. "We're leaving. You've told her more than enough."

Gnawing on her lower lip, Ann quickly restored her clothing and left without saying a word. Alone again, Maita paced in the too-small room. It had to be a dream, it had to!

No, it isn't.

Unnerved, not so much by what Ann had told her but her admittedly cloudy memories of the time she'd spent *dancing* with Kade, she dampened her cheeks once more, squared her shoulders, and walked back out into the barn. The music was just as loud, the lighting just as surreal. If anything, more sweat and hops had been added to the smell in the air, but although she'd long craved fresh oxygen, she felt embraced by the pungent mix of aromas.

Despite herself, she looked around for Kade. Instead, she spotted Rylan and Ann by the front door. Rylan was talking with a couple of stock handlers, laughing and nodding, seemingly uninterested in anything except the conversation. Ann stood by his side, her head down, hands clasped behind her almost as if kept in place by cuffs. Rylan's right arm was draped over her shoulder, his fingers stroking her throat.

"I'll walk you to your truck."

Startled, Maita whirled. Kade stood behind her and was so close she couldn't imagine how he'd entered her space without her knowing. He loomed—no other description fit. The predator had found his prey.

"It-it isn't necessary."

"You're leaving, now."

An order? No one ordered her!

"There's no reason for you to stay," he continued in his winter-night voice. "Nothing more I want to do with you here."

"*You* want to do with *me*! What the hell—"

Quick as a cougar, he reached out and gripped her jaw in his too-strong fingers. "We'll play cat and mouse later. Oh, will we! But I have another appointment tonight and want to leave you with a hint of what's to come."

Go to hell!

Instead, her arms hanging heavy at her sides, she led the way outside. As she passed Ann and her boss, they both stared at her. She read disapproval in Rylan's glare, sexual excitement in Ann's. What did Rylan have in mind for Ann?

She'd parked her pickup at the rear of the fairgrounds among the stock trucks and other dusty, battered vehicles belonging to cowboys and cowgirls. Although overhead lighting had been installed, it wasn't on, and the quarter moon did little to help her find her way. The scent of people had been replaced by dirt, oil, livestock, and hay. Despite Kade's imposing presence, she felt strangely alone. No, not really alone, she amended. She indeed shared the quiet lot with another presence, just not one she could call human and be done with definitions. Her nervousness came, not from the possibility he'd try to rape her — too many people had seen them leave together and he was a well-known figure in the community — but her inability to know how she'd react to what he had in mind.

What did he have in mind?

"I'm going to be out of town most of next week," he said when they'd reached her truck. "And you have three new horses to work with. When I return, I want to examine the merchandise, determine how fast you'll come along, and what you're capable of. Until I've spent some time with you, I can't set a time frame."

"Are you insane? I'm not—"

Not giving her time to finish, he pushed her aside, yanked open the cab door, spun her around and not quite gently deposited her belly and facedown on the seat. Using her hips as leverage, he slid her in until just her legs dangled out. Outraged, she tried to sit up. Before she could do more than bend a knee, she felt his hand between her legs. Sturdy denim provided a barrier of sorts—she shouldn't be having a sexual reaction to the dull pressure. But she did. And with his knuckles grinding against her crotch, her muscles relaxed.

"You bastard! Let me go!"

"I would if I thought you meant it," he drawled in a cocksure tone. With his free hand, he began kneading the small of her back. His fingers quickly, expertly found a conduit to her pussy.

"Stop it."

"It doesn't work that easy, my dear. I'm accustomed to initial resistance. I know how to get past that." The twin pressures increased.

"Don't," she whispered. Need made further speech difficult. Once, just once in her life she'd love to turn herself over to a man who understood her body better than she ever could. Under his control. She'd learn lessons to last a lifetime, lessons vital for surviving long, lonely nights.

"Not much of a taste of things to come," he informed her. His knuckles kneaded her sex. "But it'll give you enough to think about for the next few days. Something to anticipate."

She'd gathered enough of her wits to be asking herself how long she'd put up with this indignity when he took hold of her shoulders and helped her stand again. She couldn't muster the necessary wherewithal to face him. *Oh god! Just like that. Hot to trot. Ready. Willing?*

"It's going to be interesting," he informed her. "I can't remember the last time I went looking instead of having it come to me." He patted her ass, the pat became a massage. "Not sure why…"

Manhandled again. Manipulated.
Belatedly she realized he'd left.

Chapter Three

Kade stood back from the bound woman and appraised his handiwork. He'd blindfolded her because she'd said her lover was into sensory depravation but hadn't gagged her since communication was essential if he was going to give her the experience she was paying him for.

Nakedness brought out both the worst and best in women. As for the present subject, the implants balanced out what otherwise might be considered oversized hips. Her arms and legs were nicely muscled and contrasted well with the ropes around her wrists, ankles, and crisscrossing the always-at-attention breasts. He'd tied her to a seven-foot-high pole that ended in a horizontal T made of the same sturdy metal. He'd backed her up to the apparatus and tied her so her arms were outstretched over her head and held in place by the T. Her ankles were lashed to the bottom of the pole but loose enough so she could stand on tiptoe when the time came.

The room, part of a building he'd designed and constructed himself at a distance from the ranch house where he lived, provided him and his subjects with the privacy they needed. And if the woman turned out to be a screamer, the double insulation took care of that.

He picked up a three-foot-long metal rod.

"So tell me again, why do you want to do this with me instead of letting your *man* have all the fun?"

She turned her head in the direction of his voice. The way she kept sucking in her belly transmitted her nervousness. "He, ah, oh hell, he has more money than some foreign countries, and I don't want to screw up."

"What would he consider screwing up?"

"He, ah, he gets off on forcing climaxes. The last time we played, I came twice, but it took awhile. I thought...if you show me what works on me, I can guide him in the right direction."

"Forcing? Ropes, blindfolds, gags. What about cuffs and chains?"

She licked her lips and shifted position as best she could. "They scare me."

"Fear is a powerful aphrodisiac."

"I know." Her laugh sounded forced. "But if I'm going to lose all control over my body, the first time I want it to be with someone who doesn't matter."

With someone you're not seeing as a sugar daddy, Kade amended. He hadn't worn a watch so didn't know what time it was, but his body was telling him it wanted to be in bed alone and sleeping. However, he'd already accepted his retainer. He probably would be done with what's-her-name if he hadn't decided to join the after-rodeo celebration. If he hadn't watched Rylan's new horse trainer compete.

"On your toes," he ordered. "As high as you can get."

"What-what are you going to do?"

"Toes, now!"

Mouth sagging, she did as he'd ordered. He watched her try to keep her balance but felt nothing. Damn, he must be more tired than he'd thought. Without warning, he grabbed the inside of one naked thigh and deftly slid the rod between her legs. Then he found the hole in pole he'd tied her to and shoved the end of the pole into the hole. Hard metal now pressed against her labia and kept her on her toes. Breathing fast through her nose, she tried to turn from side to side but managed only minimal movement.

"Oh god, oh god," she kept repeating.

After giving her the better part of a minute to get used to the new level of confinement, he picked up the nipple clamps he'd selected earlier. Because he understood the seduction of the unknown, he began by caressing and pinching her breasts. "Good, good, good," she now chanted. The mantra changed to a startled and pain-touched squeak when he closed the broad-tipped clamp over her right nipple. He kept her like that for a few seconds then secured the left breast. Despite the blindfold, she tried to look down at herself.

"They're gold," he told her. "Basically expensive clothespins. They end in a loop." He flicked the clamps. "The loops are good for a number of options. Tonight I'm going to give you your choice. What'll it be? Weights or a chain?"

"Weights? No!"

"Chain then. My preference since it gives me something to play with." Despite his promise, he had to stifle a yawn. Was he getting old? Usually what he laughingly called his second job kept him in a nearly perpetual state of sexual arousal. He fastened a substantial chain to the loops and demonstrated its function by pulling on it and drawing her breasts together. He'd worked with enough silicone-enhanced breasts that he knew most had compromised sensation. Still, he was a pro at the line between pain and pleasure.

"So it's climaxes you want, is it?" he asked although he knew the answer since she'd written it on the contract he required of all his *clients*.

"Y-es."

"Clear enough. Most times I can identify each one, but why don't we each keep count, see if we come up with the same score." He picked up a lightweight whip with a good twenty strands and stroked her belly with the soft, yet strong fibers. "Before you leave, I'll give you the address of the manufacturer of this particular inducement. I haven't had any complaints with it...well, endless complaints during the actual usage but universal praise in retrospect."

"I'm scared."

"No." He punctuated the order with a slap to her captured nipples. "Never let a man see you sweat. Listen to me." He began a light, rhythmic attack on her ribs, belly, and pelvis. The blows weren't hard enough to leave marks—yet—but neither could she ignore or avoid them. "You want to play sub to your sugar daddy, you're going to need to channel fear into sexual excitement. It's the only way you're going to give him what he's paying for, got it?"

"Y-es."

"I'd like to believe you, but we aren't there yet. What I'm doing right now, softening you up, bringing you to life, is a huge part of the fun for everyone concerned." He concentrated the lashes on what of her pussy wasn't mashed against the pipe. "You're getting red here. Red means blood's pooling there, heightening the sensations to come. Go with the flow, lose yourself in you. Trust."

Trust? What a hell of a word for him to be using, he thought as he moved behind the barely writhing creature. He turned his attention to tattooing her ass. Gasping, she struggled to free herself or at least take the pressure off her straining leg muscles. What would she think if she knew how little self-control beat inside him at times like this?

Dismissing the question, he concentrated on the mechanics that now garnered him top pay in a world few people comprehended. Sweat coated her tanned body. He had to admit she had the attributes to snag whatever wealthy man she'd set her sights on. If she'd been available — like Maita — he'd happily spend the rest of the night pleasuring both of them but —

Maita? She'd be nothing like this money-grubbing bitch. A woman who got off on pitting her strength and life against rogue horses would challenge him in ways —

He'd dropped the whip and was reaching for the powerful vibrator no broad had ever been able to resist for more than a minute or two when the cell phone in his pocket began vibrating. Cursing, he moved to the far end of the room and punched send. "What?" he growled when he recognized the caller's number.

"What's the matter, good buddy? I interrupt something?" Rylan asked.

"Go to hell."

"I have no doubt of it. Question for you. You've had Ann. She's saying she doesn't like it in the ass, but I think she's playing hard to get tonight. I could just go ahead with things, but I thought I'd get a second opinion. What gets her off more, a butt plug or a cock?"

"Ask her. I'm busy."

Rylan wasn't quick to respond. "With *her*?"

"By *her* I assume you're talking about your new horse trainer." The naked woman—what was her name anyway?—had stopped shaking and was trying to listen. "If you're so interested in her, why haven't you made your move?"

"Because I need more from her than a home for my cock, and you know it. Is she there?"

"No."

Was that a sigh of relief? "A client?"

"Yes. And I don't want to have to start over with her."

"Getting to the good parts, are you?"

"I'm going to hang up."

"You sure you don't want to hear what Ann says when I tug on the little gift I gave her? Have you seen it? I had a little trouble getting it in being as it's in such a sensitive place, but she loves it now. Loves what I can do to her because of it."

Shaking off the image of slender, curious Ann with her large, juicy clit, Kade disconnected. If he hadn't worked his talent on Ann, he doubted Rylan would have looked twice at the small-breasted woman, but he and Rylan had been competitors and co-workers for so long that occasional cross-pollination, so to speak, was inevitable.

And if he made good on his promise to Maita, would Rylan try to take her from him?

What did he mean, *if*?

Without warning, a growl rumbled through him. Maita Compton was no simple bitch for hire. She was— was what?

"Where are you?" His captive sounded angry. "Who were you talking to?"

He waited until he'd joined her and taken hold of her nipple chain before answering. "No one. Now, where were we?"

* * * * *

The gelding shivered under Maita. Not taking her eyes off the first barrel, she placed one hand on the saddle horn and tightened her grip on the reins. Using her knees to guide the animal, she quickly worked him into a lope. So far the gelding kept his legs under him, proof he had his body under control. Halfway there, Maita slowed the horse to a trot and begin lifting his shoulder and positioning his front end for the turn by sliding her hand down the inside rein and picking up on it, her thumb facing upward. Use neck-rein cues, she guided the horse to a spot seven feet to the side of the barrel. When the horse's nose was even with the barrel, Maita pulled on the reins, stopping him. Horse and rider immediately backed up a couple of steps, then Maita let the horse settle for about ten seconds. The gelding's weight shifted onto his hindquarters and drove his inside hind pivot foot under his body, positioning him for a strong push off when exiting the turn.

Then, although the horse was eager to complete the turn, Maita returned him to the starting line.

"What are you doing?" Rylan asked from where he stood outside the practice corral.

"He needs to stand still," Maita explained as she stoked the horse's neck. "I want his shoulders upright and balanced, his front legs reaching and pulling the ground toward him. This way his inside pivot foot is planted under him and completing the turn becomes a piece of cake."

Rylan chuckled. "I'll take your word for it since I'm not sure I understand what you just said."

"You did your part by buying him." Maita guided the gelding over to his owner, but although she didn't plan on repeating the exercise this afternoon, she remained in the saddle. "He has great conformation."

"I know horseflesh, among other things. And it appears I knew what I was doing when I hired you."

"What'd you use, a headhunter? I was working and riding in Montana. When's the last time you were there?"

"I've never stepped foot in the state. No, not a headhunter. Let's just say an acquaintance who shares my interests told me about a sexy young woman who's fearless on horseback. When he sent me a picture, I knew I wanted you."

Maita nodded. "You're talking about interests beyond horses, aren't you?"

"You catch on quick." He took hold of the reins. "I'm playing it slow with you because the truth is, my greatest need is for someone who can work with everything from barrel horses to racers. You fit the bill."

"I know."

"Cocky, are you?"

"I know what I'm good at."

"One of the things." His attention turned to what he could see of the space between her legs. "I'm pretty content with Ann these days so wasn't in any hurry to...shall we say, bring you along." His expression sobered. "I'd hoped to keep you away from Kade, but I couldn't force you not to go to the rodeo. He saw. He liked. I knew he'd like."

No longer willing to play at word games, she dismounted and pulled off the saddle. "What are we talking about?" she demanded. "I don't like feeling like a piece of horseflesh being bid on. Bottom line, what are the two of you into?"

Approval danced in Rylan's eyes. Returning the reins to her, he briefly stroked her knuckles. "You like everything up-front, don't you?"

"When my life is involved, yes. Ann's told and shown me enough that I'm thinking you and Kade are into BDSM. I've never given it a second thought." She debated, then decided to be as honest as she required him to be. "I'm content with sex the old-fashioned way."

"What sex? Unless you're sneaking out in the middle of the night, you haven't fucked anyone since you came here."

He was right, damn it. And although she knew how to and employed the necessary techniques to scratch her itches, a dildo couldn't compete with the real thing. "You've been keeping tabs on me?"

His answer came in a slow and bold appraisal. "Why not? I enjoy it. I also know you didn't leave any stud crying in his beer when you left Montana. According to the information I have on you, you're a love 'em and leave 'em broad. How come?"

None of your damn business. "What'd you do, hire a private detective?"

"Something like that." He didn't sound embarrassed. "Look, as far as I'm concerned, your considerable physical attributes are of secondary importance. I hate admitting that because it flies in the face of my undeniable male ego, but you know what my operation is about. My reputation succeeds or fails depending on my ability to provide my customers with the finest horses their money can buy. That's where you come in."

"And because your former trainer had broken his back, you were up against it."

"You've been reading my mail."

Rylan had said little about her predecessor but from other employees, she'd learned that the Shasta Indian who'd been with him for over five years had wound up on the receiving end when a gelding he was galloping in readiness for endurance trail riding had stepped into a hole. The fall had broken the gelding's front leg, and his weight had snapped his rider's spine. Although fortunately not paralyzed, the Shasta's hell-bent-for-leather days were behind him. Now she was expected to fit the bill, something she had no qualms about doing.

"You're even better than I thought you'd be." Rylan squeezed her shoulder, the gesture speaking of approval and not an attempt to change their relationship. "I'll be honest, the first time I laid eyes on you, it took everything I had not to pull you into the relationship Ann and I have. Damn but I'd love to watch you go off."

"Crude, but I guess it's a compliment."

"It's intended as one. The thing is, much as my cock and certain aspects of my personality associated with it want to rule me, I have a greater need for what you can do for me with your clothes on than off. With your legs over a horse's back, not spread for me."

"That's it then? Our relationship defined?"

"For now."

"Works for me. Now, if you're done, I have a horse to cool down."

"In a moment." He gripped her upper arm, the firm hold reminding her of how Kade had laid claim to her, the hold of a man accustomed to dominating a woman. "Fuck anyone you want. I have a ranch full of hands more than willing to accommodate you. Just leave Kade the hell alone."

"Why?"

"He's the major leagues, Maita. You don't stand a chance against him."

* * * * *

A solitary hawk flew overhead. Whenever it changed direction, the sun turned its tail from gray to rust. Maita felt like the hawk, alone in a vast world unchanged by progress except for the ribbon of fence line. She wasn't sure whether she was still on her employer's property or had moved to land Kade Severn owned. The horse she rode, a newly gelded wild bronc from Nevada still had a lot to learn about the loss of freedom, which was why she'd decided to spend the afternoon with him away from the distraction of other animals and manmade confinement.

She felt sorry for the short, muscular bronc, but since he'd been captured, he'd had parasites removed, his hooves trimmed and been shod, an assortment of injuries treated, and an eye infection cleared up. True, he'd also lost his manhood but no longer driven by the need to impregnate meant he'd stop getting into potentially dangerous fights with other studs to say nothing of getting kicked in the face by an unreceptive mare. Once she'd finished with him, he'd go to his new owners, a couple with two horse-crazy teenage daughters. He'd spend the rest of his life being pampered instead of needing to put on enough weight each fall to survive the winter.

"It's give and take," she told the bronc whose ears immediately swiveled back to catch her words. "You're probably never going to like a saddle and bridle, unless you forget what freedom felt like. But if you'd weigh the benefits, I hope you'll decide the trade-off is worth it."

Was it? Instead of continuing her comments to the bronc, she let her thoughts return to the last few nights. Seeing Ann's clit ring had sent her mind places it never had before—only more than a captured sex organ had contributed to her restlessness. Rylan hadn't explained what he and Kade had in common, not really, and her imagination, fueled by the lack of a sex partner, had gone into high gear.

She'd long believed in and insisted on being the one on top as much as she granted the right to whoever she was sleeping with at the time. Once, when they'd both been drinking, a man had tried to tie her hands to the head of the bed they'd been using. The moment she realized she couldn't move under her own steam, she'd yelled at him to explain what the hell he thought he was doing, and that had been the end of it—and the relationship.

She didn't understand women who acted like second-class citizens to their men. The last thing she'd ever do was trade in her own last name simply because she'd slipped on a wedding ring. She couldn't imagine joint checking accounts or being called *the little woman*. If the bedroom wasn't the place for equality, what did anything else matter?

And yet didn't she love controlling animals that outweighed her many times over? She rode in rodeo bareback events because she relished pitting her strength and skill against a creature capable of killing her. To fight a man for domination, to be dominated…to lay there spread-eagled and helpless while a man poked a hole through her clit and—

"Not in this lifetime!"

Her mount sidestepped, muscles gathered for flight. As she brought the animal under control, she felt his fear and excitement through the saddle.

What was it like to helplessly fight a man's domination, to have him control her sexuality as expertly as she controlled horses? To receive instead of mete out discipline? To surrender and in her surrender experience the rewards of a man pleased with her performance?

Her cheeks felt hot. Her stretched crotch heated. Riding sometimes turned her on, and she'd learned to deal with the state either by rubbing her pussy against the saddle or pushing the horse into a gallop that effectively took her attention elsewhere. Today no one except the hawk and gelding were here to watch. She could rock back and forth, pressing cunt and inner thighs against hard, hot leather while her mind…

She was alone on the prairie, a filly feeling a brood mare's hot blood for the first time. Even as she wandered in what felt like endless restlessness, her senses remained at high alert. She needed to run until exhaustion drove her to the ground, but she held her energy in check, savoring it, feeling it on and in her entire body. *The wind fed her, its insistent heat lashing her. She studied the random, always-changing clouds and wondered what their embrace would feel like. Touching a boulder, she imagined being pressed against it, arms and legs strapped to it, her body arched over the rounded top with her breasts jutting upward, head lolling back and unable to see what her captor had in mind.*

No, he hadn't caught her yet. First came the chase, the struggle, fighting for freedom but instead finding and embracing growling sexual need.

There! On the horizon! A black-clad form on horseback, a large man with a midnight stallion under him. The horse whinnied and charged. Screaming, she broke into a frantic run. Even as she sought even ground, she looked over her shoulder. The man now worked a lasso over his head, his free hand resting on his thigh because the stallion needed no guiding. Despite her fear-lathered pace, she couldn't outrun her pursuer.

She sensed the lasso circling above her, felt it kiss her cheek before closing around her arms and pinning them to her side. The stallion stopped abruptly. Yanked backward, she landed first on her ass, then struck the back of her head on the ground. By the time she regained consciousness, the cowboy had wrapped the lasso around and around her upper body and used another rope to lash her legs together.

"Mine," he said. "Mine to do what I want with."

She couldn't bring his features into focus, but her breasts knew the feel of this man's touch.

Kade Severn.

* * * * *

Transporting enough broncs and bulls to supply a three-day rodeo five hundred miles away had left Kade tired, dirty, and seriously wondering why in the hell he'd gotten into the business. True, he always felt this way by the time he dragged his sorry ass home, but this time the effort had sucked more than usual out of him.

"You're getting old," he muttered as he watched his hands unload the last of the horses. He didn't understand how the broncs had enough energy to charge around their pasture after being cooped up all day. If it was him, he'd be drinking from the just-filled water trough before filling his belly from the nearby piles of hay. Unfortunately, he had no choice but to log some time in his office catching up on paperwork and responding to what he had no doubt would be a small mountain of correspondence from the organizers of the next three or four rodeos he'd contracted for.

Another woman client would soon be arriving. By then he'd be more than ready for a change of pace—a change guaranteed to satisfy both of them but in different ways. He'd received a number of offers of female companionship over the course of the rodeo, but for some damn reason, he'd turned them down.

"Just getting myself primed for you, whoever you are," he said to the upcoming client. What the hell was it she wanted anyway? He thought she'd said her boss had recommended him, and she was willing to do whatever it took to get the promotion. "We'll see if you've changed your tune by the time I'm done with you," he added although the truth was, he didn't give a damn.

"You want us to get started on the steering on the stake truck?" his foreman asked as the weary hands started toward the bunkhouse.

"It'll wait until tomorrow. I'll tell you what. After everyone gets cleaned up, see if they want to go into town. I'll buy the first two rounds."

"What do you mean, if?"

Kade was still smiling in response to his foreman's grin when he spotted someone on horseback coming down the long gravel drive leading from the county road. Because he was looking into the sun, at first he thought it was one of the area's teens. Then his well-developed senses said this was no adolescent boy.

Maita rode a scruffy, long-haired stub of a horse he recognized as one of the creatures who'd grown up wild on government land. Rylan occasionally agreed to gentle one of those animals but only for clients willing to pay his fees. It wasn't any of Kade's damn business, but the way he looked at it, Maita's talents—from what he'd seen of her skill at the rodeo, he knew they were considerable— were better used on horses with a chance of earning back their investment. Still, seeing her cleaned his system of all weariness.

She rode as if she and the horse shared the same set of muscles. Because he knew horsemanship, he knew she was in tune with her mount's every mood and instinct, no easy task since horses' brains regularly short-circuited. She could fall asleep in the saddle and still know a horse was going to buck before the animal did itself. She appeared more horse than human, an extension of the creature under her.

He wished he was the one under her—or even better, her under him.

"Taking a busman's holiday are you?" he asked when she was close enough for them to carry on a conversation. "It's your day off but instead of getting your nails done, you've come to see what your boss's neighbor's operation is like?"

"It isn't my day off. Blue needs all the riding time I can give him."

"And you decided to come here?" He hadn't shaved since at least yesterday and undoubtedly smelled like the back of a stock truck. No wonder she was keeping her distance—unless something else was responsible. The possibilities for that *something* intrigued him. He'd never take her for shy or unsure, but their brief time together hadn't told him anything about her interest in what he offered. Well, not much.

"I wasn't thinking about my destination." She indicated the nearby trucks. "You just got back?"

"About an hour ago. I was going to go in for something to drink. You want to join me? How is Blue about being left tied?"

"He'll take it for a little while." Her expression turned introspective. Was she pondering whether she'd be safe with him? He could point out they were hardly alone but decided to let her make the decision. Besides, maybe she didn't give a damn about safe. He could dream.

With a shrug, she tossed the reins to him and dismounted. He stood close enough that he could have run his hands over her descending thighs and buttocks but forced himself not to. His thoughts fixed on the only other time he'd seen her ride. Bareback bronc riding was a man's sport, raw and dangerous. But she'd not only entered a competition where death sometimes happened—she'd excelled.

"Did he fight you?" He indicated Blue.

"No. By the time I got him, he'd learned fighting won't get him anywhere." She stroked the ugly beast's nose. "We've been working on trust."

He specialized in trust. Trust mixed with resistance, fear, and desire. How would she respond?

"What would he do if you took the ropes off him?"

"I'm not taking the chance, not yet."

"Wise decision. What's your usual procedure? Teaching a wild animal he wants what you offer more than the alternative even if it means giving up his freedom?"

Her gray-eyed gaze said she understood he wasn't talking about horseflesh anymore. "Every horse has different priorities, different needs. The same techniques don't work for all of them."

"Spoken like a pro. Come on." He nodded at the ranch house. "I'm offering beer. Cold."

* * * * *

She hadn't been roped. No tethers circled her ankles.

Still, Maita admitted as Kade handed her a frosty mug, it had been an intriguing if unsettling fantasy. When they reached the front porch, he'd invited her inside, but she needed to keep an eye on Blue so had said she'd wait for him on the porch. He'd agreed, explained he needed to check a few things in his office but wouldn't be long. She'd told him not to hurry, but he'd explained he'd just as soon sit in his own chair on his own land and talk to a neighbor than anything else. She'd laughed and nodded and hadn't said anything about not knowing what it felt like to own a single square inch of land but wanting that—someday.

He smelled of honest work. Dust coated his hair, and his jeans were stained and faded. He more than needed a shave, but from the way he now sprawled in the hand-carved wooden chair, she wondered if he might fall asleep before he could make his way into a shower. With his eyes closed and his body limp, she could study his form and maybe begin to understand the fascination he held for her.

"Long trip?" she asked after giving him time to down most of his beer.

"Long and intense. I feel like a one-armed paper hanger during a rodeo with everyone coming to me at once."

"Do you like what you do?"

He looked at her, his attention, she believed, torn between an adequate answer and her as a human being, a woman. She didn't know how to dress for a man, how to offer one anything beyond her body. Today, she wished she had on something other than horse-scented jeans and a wrinkled shirt.

No, the truth was, she want to be naked.

"Yes." He drawled the word. "I like what I do."

"The headaches?"

"Yeah."

"The rules and regulations, dealing with rodeo committees that don't always know what they want and either expect you to handle it all or think they're calling the shots? Being responsible for rogue horses and bulls who'd rather kill you than eat?"

"The stock's not much of a hassle if you know how to treat them."

"Treat?" She winked in the way of one insider to another. "Hell, as long as we don't put a rope on a rogue horse, he's a pussycat, and if you leave a bull alone, he'll do the same to you."

"Just don't tell the press or fans or I'm out of business." He focused his attention on her. "Why do you put yourself on a bareback bronc? Damn it, you know he'll turn himself inside out trying to get rid of you."

"I want to see if he can do it."

"Don't you mean you want to find out which of you will win the battle?"

"Something like that." She studied the droplets sliding down the outside of her glass but didn't really see them. She wasn't much good at small talk, undoubtedly the result of her childhood, but although her skin felt lightning-charged this close to Kade, she had no desire to do anything except what she was—for a while at least. "Rylan told me to leave you alone."

"Did he?" Looking not at all surprised, Kade leaned back and rested his boots on the porch railing. Even relaxed, his thigh and calf muscles remained hard. "Then you shouldn't be here."

"No one tells me what to do."

"Ever?"

Although he'd only glanced at her, she knew the question hadn't been casual. "Not anymore."

"But once? When and under what circumstances?"

"I'm not going there," she told him.

"I'll accept that, for now."

But you have ways of getting the truth out of me? "Why did Rylan say what he did?"

"Because I'm a Brahma bull, Maita. A woman would be a fool to trust me."

She scooted her chair closer to the railing and used it as an elevated footrest like he had. "I'm not afraid."

"Of anything?"

Not anymore. "Not that I can think of."

"Have you ever been afraid of yourself?"

The question circled them and ignited a small fire under her breastbone. She finished her beer and kept her attention on Blue who was starting to get restless. "Explain," she said.

"Testing a woman's limits is part of what I'm about, Maita. It's engrained in my nature—or maybe I should say it developed over the years."

"Interesting." The fire kicked up a notch, and she worked at not moving. "So where do you find the women you…test? Maybe you advertise in the local paper."

"Not a large enough drawing area." He indicated seemingly endless acres of nothing. "Advertising isn't necessary because of word of mouth."

"You're talking about a lifestyle I've never been interested in."

"You're wrong."

She'd once been bitten by a dog who'd announced his aggression with a low, throaty growl she hadn't paid enough advance attention to, but the lesson had remained. Kade had just issued his own warning. "What makes you say that?"

"Instinct." He stood up. "I'm what some people call a dom," he explained. "In the world of submission and control, I control, but it goes beyond the usual BDSM game. I'm good at what I do, damn good."

"Congratulations." A trickle of sweat ran down the small of her back.

After glancing at Blue, he closed the distance between them until his jeans brushed her elevated thighs. "You interest me, Maita. Not just because you remind me of a wild horse, and I love throwing a rope on one for the first time, but because you're a mix I haven't seen before. Because I don't understand you, and that doesn't often happen."

She'd known he was going to touch her, but damn it, why hadn't he telegraphed his intention? The light pressure on her calf through the denim barely registered. Still she felt the contact all the way up her legs.

"When you're ready, I'll teach you about your body," he promised and threatened. "Introduce you to things about it you never knew. Most women who come to me— hell, all of them—know what they want. I fulfill their requests." He pressed his palm against her chin bone and kept his attention on her eyes. "But you don't yet know what you want and need from me so I'm going to offer you several options."

"How generous." Although she'd left her legs slightly parted and her crotch semi-accessible, she refused to back down from his challenge. Besides, so far the challenge to anything except her nervous system was minimal.

Blue whinnied and stomped.

"Your time here is short," Kade said. "And I have a lot to do before my next *customer* arrives."

Although she could have used his comment to end whatever the hell was going on, she didn't move. "What customer?"

"Female, of course. She's jockeying for a promotion, and because I've serviced a couple of her boss's other female employees, I know what he wants. If you want to

57

watch, you're welcome to. In fact—" he increased the pressure on her leg, "—I dare you to."

Watch what? The silent question stirred her senses.

"No, *dare* isn't the operant word after all. I strongly suggest it because it'll give you a fair idea of what to expect from me."

"Who says I want anything from you?"

His smile began and ended with his mouth. "You will. Believe me, you will." He punctuated his comment by sliding his hand to the inside of her leg. Slow, so slow she thought she might scream, his fingers inched higher and higher, nearing her warm cave. "So, we'll agree that you'll show up back here after dark. You won't come to the house but continue on the county road until the next turnoff. That'll take you to what from the outside looks like a large stone storage building. When you get there, knock." He demonstrated by tapping her crotch once, twice, three times.

"Who will be there?" Her mouth felt dry.

"Just me and a woman."

His hand returned to her inner thigh, cradling and stroking it much as a loving owner might reassure a nervous horse. "Now to your and my first session. I'm not going to charge so don't worry about being able to afford me."

Don't move. Don't let him see you sweat. "Who says I want to any sessions?"

"You won't know unless you try, will you? Of course if you're afraid—"

"I'm not!" *The years of fear are behind me.*

"Good. To give you some idea of what you might expect, a particularly favorite technique of mine involves a spreader bar fixed to your ankles and spreading your legs so the playground's right where I need it." He cupped his hand over her crotch. She waited, silently willing him to remove it before she forgot what the hell she was suppose to do with the rest of the day, but he kept his large paw in place. "Your hands will be tied behind you but up, not down, and back over your head which forces you to lean forward. Gag is optional — at least on my part."

"Optional!" Furious, she pushed herself to her feet which dislodged him but left her pussy imprinted with his touch. "You're out of your fucking, ever-loving mind! If you think I'm going to let you hogtie me, you're sick."

Smiling with his mouth again, he folded his arms across his chest. "Righteous indignation. I was wondering when you'd play that card."

"You can hardly blame me."

"Perhaps not, but I was hoping for better."

She should leave, damn it. "Sorry if I don't live up to your expectations," she shot at him then winced because she sounded as if she'd had her pride wounded. Damn it, the man made her crazy!

Crazy with wanting what he's offering?

Well, maybe.

"So, for comparison sake," she said, "if I'm not interested in technique number one, what else do you have up your sleeve?"

"Who says I'll be wearing a sleeve?" he drawled. "Don't worry about getting bored. My repertoire is damn near endless, but you mentioned an intriguing possibility when you brought up hogtying."

"I can hardly wait to hear about it." She hoped she'd injected enough sarcasm in her voice to mask her fear and interest.

He'd backed off when she'd stormed to her feet, but now his long legs ate up all but a couple of inches of the space between them. He loomed. "I prefer rope to chains because there's some play in rope. So you want the details, do you? Far be it from me to disappoint a woman. Getting back to hogtie, we'll start out basic with your knees bent and ankles pulled as close to your ass as you can stand. From the looks of you, you're flexible."

"I am." She kept her tone neutral.

"Can you make your elbows touch behind your back?"

"I've never tried."

"We will—or rather, I will, since I'll be calling the shots. Picture yourself on your side, hands behind you and nearly touching your tethered feet, right where I want you. Next I'll probably put a gag on you, a little custom-made number with a hook at the back of your head. When I slip a rope through the hook and tie it to the ankle tie, I can force your neck back. Makes for a long, clean line of exposed flesh from knee to chin, not that you'll be in a position to appreciate the effect."

"Take pictures," she snapped to counter the heat crawling over her throat. Unfortunately, the attempt didn't work.

"I usually do." He rubbed his chin, indicating contemplation. "I'm trying to think whether I've given you an accurate description. You'll be naked of course with your breasts accessible. I want to see your breasts, feel them, put my stamp on them."

Like a brand? Although she was shaken, instead of being horrified by the idea of having some man place his brand on her, her imagination pushed into overload.

"I know what you're thinking, Maita. Trying to anticipate what's meant by nipple play. But because you're a virgin to bondage, all you have to go by is your imagination. Of course, after tonight you'll have a better idea. Much better."

"You're damn cocky, you know it." If she so much as moved a muscle, he'd think he'd won this round—intimidated her—and her years of being intimidated were behind her.

"Not cocky. An expert." With a nod, he turned away and picked up the empty mugs. "You have a horse waiting for you, an animal to tame. When you're ready for me to do the same to you, come back."

Chapter Four

The woman was stunning. Except for a thin bikini line, her tan covered every inch of flesh. He wished he'd opted for white rope to contrast with her bronzed flesh, but because planning was essential to success, he'd decided to put her in stocks before he'd met her. When she'd shown up, Lisa whatever her last name was, had exhibited defiance and bravado. He'd let her play her game while they went through introductions and the ground rules were laid out. Even when he'd told her to take off her shoes and underpants, she'd retained an admirable self-confidence.

Then he'd stepped behind her, snaked his arm around her neck and pulled her against him. Before she could so much as think about regaining her balance, he yanked up on her short skirt and unceremoniously buried a thumb in her pussy.

Now he had her naked and on her knees, her feet in stocks that forced her weight onto her knees. He'd placed Styrofoam under her so she could handle the position for a while and pulled her arms back and into more wooden stocks that forced her to arch her spine. He hadn't gagged her, yet, because he didn't yet know enough about her to read her body language, but if she didn't quit asking stupid questions about what he had in mind and reminding him of how important she was to her employer, he would.

Her long, bleached blonde hair hung over her cheeks. As he'd suspected, her breasts weren't entirely her own, but he could work around that. Feeling nothing between his own legs, he secured small clamps to her nipples and hung a weight from each one.

"Damn, damn, damn," she hissed.

You ain't seen nothing yet.

Neither had Maita, he admitted. His reaction surprised him since even as he'd issued his invitation earlier, he'd told himself it didn't matter if she didn't show up.

But it did. She did.

Maita rode the short, stocky horse as if she'd been born to a saddle, and although Blue had accepted her weight without objection, he'd easily made the leap between what she looked like riding away from him and her slight, strong body clinging to the whirling devil that had been one of his bareback broncs.

His horses could kill her.

"I can't take this much longer," Lisa whined.

Cursing to himself, Kade concentrated on his latest paycheck. Still, as he guided a sleek metal hook into her cunt and held it in place via a chain around her neck, he continued to feel both physically and emotionally removed from what he was doing—a new experience. He should have put Lisa off until tomorrow after he'd had time to regroup and recover from the just-finished rodeo. Another night's sleep and he'd be more than ready to give Lisa—and himself—a ride for their money.

Because he knew how to do his job, he carefully cinched the hook tight against and in Lisa's lush body without hurting her. He stroked her breasts, careful not to touch her trapped and sensitive nipples.

"He wants you hot to trot," he explained, speaking of Lisa's insanely wealthy employer. "You'll never know when he'll order you to meet him at his place, and you're not going to know what to expect once you get there. But you can anticipate." Making his point, he picked up an electric vibrator, turned it on, and pressed it against the full curve of Lisa's breast. She jumped and cursed, what he could see of her fingers beneath the stocks widespread and tense. "He's a bastard, but he rewards his bitches—if they please him."

Changing tactics, he ran the humming tool between the luscious breasts and headed for her navel. She tried to escape the invasion, but he'd left her with no freedom.

She belonged to him, had become his toy, his fantasy.

Only, tonight, he'd probably get as much enjoyment out of sheering a sheep.

"Damn, damn, damn," Lisa whimpered. "I can't—I can't."

"Yes." He ran the vibrator over her belly, pressed it against her mons, headed unerringly for her clit. "You can. And the more you bellow and beg, the more he'll reward you. Get used to being called a bitch. He gets off on it."

Before he could decide what do to next—something that hadn't happened to him in years—he heard the knock. Suddenly, his quivering and helpless subject meant nothing to him. Leaving the vibrator to thump against the floor, he forced himself to walk slowly to the door. Just before opening it, he turned off the overhead light, leaving a small floor lamp to bathe Lisa's body in muted light.

"You came," he said to the slight form outside.

"I came."

"Why?"

"I don't know. Don't ask."

"All right." *For now.* "We've started. You can watch. And if you want to get involved, let me know."

Maita exhaled. "I wouldn't know what to do."

"You'll learn." Earlier, he'd told himself he wasn't going to touch her, but he must not have listened because now he saw nothing wrong with putting his arm around her waist and holding her against him before guiding her to a wall. From the sound her shoes made on the carpeted floor, he knew she'd changed out of her riding boots. Instead of her usual jeans, white shorts clung to her flat belly and firm, rounded ass. Her blouse felt like silk against his skin.

"What's going on?" Lisa demanded. "Who's she?"

"It doesn't matter. You're never going to see her again." *But I am.* Although he knew better, knew Maita had every right to plant a knee between his legs, he again wrapped an arm around her until she looked up at him, and then kissed her—long and hard enough for both of them to remember. He couldn't recall the last time he'd kissed a woman.

"Sorry about the interruption," he told Lisa when he'd again knelt before her and picked up the vibrator. "Now, where were we?"

Had Kade fucked the gorgeous blonde before imprisoning her and playing with her?

It didn't matter, Maita insisted as she watched him stoke the woman's cunt with the large, powerful vibrator. What the two of them did was none of her business. Besides, she shouldn't be here.

But she was.

Still not believing she'd entered this room of her own free will, Maita sank to the floor and leaned against the wall. All afternoon she'd told herself she had no intention of satisfying her curiosity about Kade's activities, if that's what he called them. Then, after she'd finished work, and showered and washed her hair, she'd stood naked before the narrow mirror behind the door of the cabin her employer had provided. For a while she'd simply studied her image, wondering what Kade would think of her lean, muscled form. Would he want to touch her, explore her, handle her as she handled a horse? Would his expert hands roam appraisingly over her, turning from professional detachment to something purely male?

And how would she respond?

She hadn't found the answer then and sitting here listening to the naked blonde breathe in quick sobs wasn't improving matters — unless getting turned on counted.

The woman had something rammed into her pussy. Because the lighting didn't come close to killing the shadows, she wasn't sure what it was, but it put her in mind of an oversized fishing hook. Undoubtedly, it had no barbed end. If what was inside her was as smooth as the rest of the contraption, it had to feel delicious — a hard, artificial cock.

Kade might have put it there after securing the woman's wrists and ankles in the wooden stocks. Had she taken off her own clothes and willingly placed herself so her limbs fit in their constraints, or had she fought? Had Kade manhandled her into submission, pitting his strength against hers until he won the battle?

No matter. He'd rendered her as helpless as a horse or cow in a squeeze chute. Until he decided to free the blonde with the fake boobs, she belonged to him.

"My breasts, my breasts," the woman chanted. She rocked her upper body from side to side which caused the weights on her nipples to bounce and jiggle. "Hurts!"

"Get used to it, bitch!" Kade barked. "He gets off on pain."

"No, no, no! I can't—I can't."

"Yes, you can."

Maita shook, her body felt alive with a mix of disbelief and anticipation. What would Kade do next? And if she was his prisoner instead of this whimpering—

Keeping the vibrator between the woman's legs, Kade practically ripped off the nipple clamps. The woman screamed. Her head fell forward as she tried to look down at herself. His movements quick and practiced, Kade sprang to his feet, grabbed something black off the floor and used the woman's hair to pull her head back. Although she tried to jerk free, he easily blindfolded her.

"Is it better this way, Lisa?" he asked. "Maybe it's easier if you can't see what I have in mind."

Kade was speaking to Lisa, not her. Still, Maita tried to imagine what it would be like deprived of sight while some man—no, not just any man—laid claim to her.

Kade Severn represented strength and stability. In a sport filled with losers and a handful of winners whose time of victory lasted only until the next ride, he supplied the creatures necessary for rodeos to take place and did so competently and humanely. But in the past few minutes, he'd proven himself as much more than just a stock contractor. He controlled women in a way she'd never comprehended or wanted.

Did she now?

No longer were Lisa's limbs the ones being held fast. In her mind, Maita took the other woman's place. She felt cool air on her naked breasts and belly, felt the strain in her legs, shoulders, and arms and fought to free herself from the hard constraints. Her breasts burned from the recently removed clamps, and her pussy lapped at what had been placed in it.

As Kade moved the hook to the side and slid his finger in next to the steel intrusion, Maita's clit clenched and hardened. She felt each commanding stroke, she shuddered as Kade first pinched her breast and then caught it in his large, knowing hand.

He now caressed *her* thighs and waist, closed his fingers around *her* throat and held *her* life in his strength. She, who'd long prided herself on her freedom and independence, became a strong man's possession. In some respects, she reverted back to the small and helpless child she'd been so many years ago. But there was a vital difference. As a child she'd had no comprehension of what it meant to be a woman and a sexual being. Now she did.

As surely as if she'd been run down and roped, she had no choice but to endure and revel in her master's command. Heat grew and spread throughout her, numbing her fingers and toes and turning her pussy into molten lava.

Not caring what he'd think, she unzipped her shorts and thrust her hand between her legs. In her imagination, the hand became his. *His* fingers explored her labia, teasing and testing them before gripping them between thumb and forefinger and rolling the loose, hot flesh back and forth. He found the trigger to release her sex fluids. Once the dam had been sprung, it flowed unchecked, endless lubrication readying her cunt to house his cock.

His cock instead of fingers and foreign objects! His body pressed to hers, belly to belly and her breasts flattened against him.

He might take her from the rear by placing her facedown on a bed or positioning her doggy style on the floor. Whatever his choice, his pleasure, her cunt would suck him deep, deep into her, and she'd clamp her muscles around him and keep him there until she climaxed.

Climax? No, not yet, she ordered although masturbating was bringing her close. Lisa's sounds alternated between pleasure-screams and exhausted whimpers as her forced climax went on and on. Even as she stroked and teased her own clit, Maita envied the noisy woman. At the same time Kade's insistence on a prolonged sexual explosion unnerved her. Lisa had had enough. She couldn't take much more.

Neither could she.

Under her own relentless assault, Maita's muscles clenched and unclenched. She felt herself drawing upward and into herself, her body tight and shaking all at once, heat stroking her flesh. In her imagination, she'd been stripped naked and existed in raw woman form. Nothing mattered except sensuality and pleasure.

Her climaxes had always been inwardly directed, near silent affairs designed to protect her at her most vulnerable. Nothing changed in the dimly lit room as a combination of self-work and Lisa's bellowing example threw her over the edge. Maita sheltered and tortured her cunt, pushed it until it could take no more—until it brought her lonely pleasure.

* * * * *

Maita smelled of sex. But her expression gave away nothing as she walked over to him and Lisa. Because he'd had enough of listening to Lisa beg for mercy, Kade had stopped playing with her and removed the hook by the time Maita joined them. Lisa sagged in her bonds.

"Was it worth it?" Maita asked and began rubbing Lisa's shoulders to ease his captive's discomfort. "Was the pleasure worth the pain?"

"God, yes."

"And you'd do it again?"

"Not tonight." Lisa gave a shaky laugh. "But ask me again once I've rested."

He unlocked the padlocks and separated the sections of stocks so Lisa could free herself. Apparently uninterested in putting an end to her naked state, Lisa sat on the carpet, removed her blindfold, and touched the marks the wood had left on her ankles.

"Forget my damn boss," she said. "I'm quitting my job and coming to work for you. You wouldn't even have to pay me, just bring me in here every few days."

"Can you load Brahmas or calculate how much feed to order or hire and fire wranglers?"

"Shit, no. But I'd keep you happy." Lisa acknowledged Maita for the first time. "Unless I'm too late and you're already being satisfied by her."

"No," Kade and Maita said at the same time.

"I just met him," Maita explained. "He invited me to watch tonight. I hope you don't mind."

Lisa laughed. "The truth? I was much too self-involved to give a damn what else was going on. So." Lisa turned her attention back to him. "This is what I have to get used to if I'm going to be allowed to climb to the top of the corporate ladder?"

"In that corporation and with that particular boss, yes."

* * * * *

"Do you think she'll do it?" Maita asked once Lisa had dressed and left.

"What?" Kade asked. "Stay with her job?"

"Yes. How often does this go on in the corporate world?"

Although he hadn't finished putting away his *equipment*, Kade left what he was doing and joined Maita who'd perched on the edge of the narrow bed that served as one of his props. When he sat down, his weight caused her to lean toward him, unfortunately not close enough so they touched. He tried not to look at her thighs or imagine what her legs under the spotless shorts would feel like.

"Not much, I hope," he admitted. "I don't like the idea of companies acting as fronts for this shit."

"But you benefit from the desire for that kind of behavior. I'd think you'd encourage—"

"What people do in their own worlds isn't my business." His tone sounded sharper than he'd intended but damn it, Maita was touching on something he didn't much like examining and particularly not tonight. "I provide a service. If they want it, fine. If not, fine."

She continued studying him. Her hands remained folded loosely in her lap, telling him nothing about what she was thinking, whether she'd judged him or what conclusion she'd come to.

"It's more than a service," she pointed out. "You're hardly supplying office furniture."

He laughed, an open and spontaneous reaction. "True. So?"

She boldly met his gaze. "Are you asking if I want to experience what Lisa did? I haven't decided."

"Are you afraid of anything?"

"Not anymore," she said and leaned back on the bed, supporting her upper body with her elbows. She looked so vulnerable and open, accessible. But much as he ached to touch her, he didn't.

"But once?" he prodded.

Again her attention latched onto him, making him glad for the dim lighting. "You aren't the only one who doesn't want to talk about certain things, all right."

Although she'd spoken softly, he clearly heard the *we're not going there* behind the words. "What about when you're in a chute sitting on the back of some horse who'd love to bash in your skull?" he demanded. "In the seconds before the gate opens, your heart rate remains normal? You aren't so much as apprehensive?"

She stretched out and laced her hands behind her head. Despite her deceptively casual stance, he had no doubt she'd react to any move on his part. Her body language served as a silent message—*don't step over the line.*

"I'd be a damn idiot if I thought I was immune to getting hurt," she said. "A healthy dose of caution keeps my skull intact. Besides, if a bronc's hooves find my head, it's an accident, not deliberate like it is with a bull."

"In other words, you stick to horses because they're prey animals, not predator. They're ruled by flight, not fight."

"And because they smell better than bulls."

"It's a matter of opinion. Having been up close and personal to the ass end of both, I prefer neither."

Maita chuckled, the sound sliding over his belly and touching his already erect cock. "Good point. Do you ever compete?" she asked.

"Used to. Now I'm too old."

"No, you're not. Kade, I pay my entry fees because I get high on pitting myself against something physical and because, so far, I haven't been hurt bad enough to have a good reason to quit. If I can be honest, so can you."

She'd seen past the BS he'd tried to hand her. He'd be wise to remember her ability to cut through to the truth of a person. "I'm a businessman," he told her. "I've been around the rodeo world for years and seen it both make people rich and destroy them. I opted for rich — particularly after I broke my knee."

She winced but didn't offer sympathy probably because in her book people got what they deserved — adults anyway. "You want to tell me what happened?" she asked.

I'd rather fuck both our brains out. Shaken because he truly wanted to have sex with her, not repeat what he'd done to Lisa, he forced himself to concentrate on providing her with a decent answer. Keeping his tone level, he sketched the innocent summer day of his twenty-second year when the brash, testosterone-laden buck he'd once been had climbed onto the back of a Brahma innocuously named Sammy Q. His head and other parts of his anatomy had been full of memories of the night before spent at a bar and the woman he'd taken back to the trailer he'd hauled to this particular rodeo, the hours spent lost in her body.

"I didn't have my mind on business," he told Maita. "I should have concentrated on my rope work, but I didn't."

"And when you were thrown, your hand got hung up?"

He stretched out on his side beside her and supported his upper body with his bent arm so he could look down at her. "Yeah. I did the whole rag doll thing. Finally the clowns freed me, but by then I'd hit the fence a few times and been knocked out. To finish the job, Sammy stepped on my knee."

She touched the side of his neck. "Which one?"

"Right."

"You can walk all right, can't you?" Her fingers remained on him.

"The only time it bothers me is if I put too much strain on it. It gets tired easier than the rest of me."

"And it's not much good for clamping around a bull's ribs, is it?"

"Not worth a damn."

Despite the throb in his cock, he'd have stayed like he was, letting her feather her fingers over his flesh for as long as she wanted. But that was before she wrapped her arms around his neck and pulled him down onto her. Her mouth found his, soft and full, her lips slightly parted.

Something stirred inside him, something separate from his so-ready cock. He didn't want to examine the new reaction. Hell, he had no interest in acknowledging it.

Concentrating on familiar territory, he bracketed his body over hers and held her head in place to deepen their kiss. She gave his tongue entrance, arching toward him despite the weight of his body. They remained unmoving except for their mouths, the contact shaking him. He understood laying claim to a woman and the hard, familiar ache of relentless need. Having the woman free to give and give and give... How long had it been since he'd experienced this?

"How do you do it?" she whispered. "Unless you finish by fucking your clients, how do you handle your reactions?" She lifted her hips off the bed and ground her thighs against his cock for emphasis. "You're turned on. You can't just jerk off time and time again."

He didn't often. With rodeo groupies free for the asking, frustration seldom lasted long. He told her that, then tried to gage her reaction. "I limit my *clients*," he heard himself say. "By controlling the sessions, I control me."

"From what?"

I don't know! "Do you want to fuck or not?" he snapped. "It's been a long day."

"Yeah." She made a small sound, maybe a sigh. "I want to fuck."

He'd wanted to bed her since the day they met, but her strangely unenthusiastic response bothered him. If he didn't have his starving libido to deal with, he'd make her explain what she was thinking about. However...

Lessons learned from countless experiences kicked in. He began by rolling off her and positioning himself on his knees next to her. She started to reach for him, but although he wanted—needed—her touch, he took hold of her wrists and positioned her arms above her head.

"The whole submissive thing," she whispered. "Is sex with you always like that?"

Half angry, he squeezed her breasts through blouse and bra. "What the hell do you care about always? This is now."

Her shrug galled him almost as much as her small, knowing smile did. Determined to wipe it off her mouth, he deftly unbuttoned her blouse and pulled it away from the lush body underneath. He'd seen countless breasts and midsections and had long ago stopped trying to keep them separate in his mind. This body, however, would remain with him.

Rolling her away from him, he drew an arm out of one sleeve, unfastened her bra, and then placed her on her belly. He had to pull her other arm behind her to finish the undressing and nearly apologized for causing her discomfort. Instead, he once again placed her arms over her head and started walking his fingers over her shoulder blades and spine. The snug shorts waistband stopped his exploration. He leaned low over her and used his tongue to bathe the base of her spine.

"Oh god," she whimpered. "It feels so good."

Yes, he admitted. *It did.*

By turn he lapped at the wonderfully soft flesh and pressed his thumbs into the tiny hollow. In his mind, he reached through flesh, bone, and muscle to her cunt. She twitched under him and breathed as if preparing for a race. Her skin felt flawless. She'd been made for beds and sex, not risking her life on the back of some damn powerful animal.

Most times he had little knowledge of and even less interest in what *his* women did with the rest of their lives. Knowing as much about Maita as he did complicated things. Confused by his reaction to the complexity, he allowed his fingers and now the heel of his hand to transmit his emotions via ever-greater pressure. Her twitching increased. She now sounded as if the race had begun.

"Kade!" She braced her arms under herself and pushed away. "You're hurting—"

"You don't know the meaning of the word!" Acting on instinct and self-training, he dropped on top of her and pinned her to the firm mattress. "You're turned on. Hell, we both are."

Although surely she knew how useless it was, she continued to struggle. "You revved me up, you bastard! Now either treat me like an equal or get the hell off me!"

Not tonight. Not before we've burned each other out.

She tried to kick him. "Why the hell do you have to be so damn strong?"

Determined not to go there, he switched tactics. Taking his time and studying her reaction, he lifted himself off her but kept a hand on the middle of her back. "Stay there," he ordered. After patting her on the ass, he slipped off the bed and undressed. Because he'd left her with her head turned away from him, she couldn't see what he was doing, but she must have heard the zipper.

Back with her, he rolled her onto her back. Her eyes widened and ran slowly over him, touching him with heat and shared desire. Licking her lips, she repositioned her arms over her head. "Take me," she quipped. "I'm yours."

"For tonight."

"Yes, for tonight."

He wanted to draw out the process, but the moment he took hold of the button on her shorts, he knew only one speed. Almost before he'd finished unzipping her, he yanked the sturdy white fabric down over her hips. She helped as best she could by lifting her lower body and separating her legs. His nails lightly raked her flanks in his haste to rid her of her nearly nothing underpants.

Maita, naked. On his bed. In the house he'd built for the lessons of domination. He couldn't stop staring at her, both grateful for the lighting that kept his own features in shadow and wanting to see her in full daylight.

He'd keep her here until morning, then take her outside and have her stand with the sun beating down and kissing her with heat, the image burying itself deep in him. He needed to watch her reaction to a breeze on her naked skin, to study the nuances of movement as she turned for him, as she reached deep into his mind and heart and soul and learned what he wanted of her.

But if the sunlight bathed her, it would do the same to him, and he needed darkness. He wanted no more of her probing eyes searching his for the truth of him.

Angry at both of them, he slid her around until she was in the middle of the bed, then again flipped her unceremoniously onto her belly. As she'd done before, she tried to look at him, but this time when he pressed her flat against the mattress, she stayed where she was. She gripped the sheet.

Her fingers became his barometer. His aching cock and heated belly told him more than he needed to know about his own readiness for sex.

In his fantasies, he licked women to climax, but the actual act was too intimate. Better to allow an object to become his tongue, emotionally safer. Drawing once more on experience, he separated her legs. He went unerringly to her pussy, collected some of her juice and lubricated her from mons to asshole. Her knuckles whitened. If her nails had been longer, she might have ripped the fabric. She again lifted her buttocks toward him, which pressed her head against the bed and stopped his concerns about her being able to watch him.

"You don't... You go right for the kill, don't you?"

"Why not?" He slapped her cheeks. "It works."

When she didn't respond to the light slap, he spread her buttocks which increased his access to her pussy. Much as he'd like to see her reaction to a butt plug, he couldn't bring himself to leave her long enough to select one. Besides, he wanted to feel her — *he*.

With his forefinger poised at the entrance to her rectum, he changed his mind although in truth he didn't remember making a conscious decision. Rather, he went with instinct, dipping into her pussy, feeling her wet heat, her cunt muscles clenching his finger and trying to suck it deeper.

She moaned, the sound muffled. She presented him with more of her sex by spreading her legs further and bending her knees slightly. Another time, he'd splay her — or ask her to splay herself — so he could study everything. Tonight, however, he needed to lose himself in her sex.

Not yet ready for the act of surrender and, yes, trust, he worked his middle finger in next to the first and simply experienced as her muscles pressed his digits together. Soft, warm, wet, her delicate flesh nevertheless might swallow him.

Could his cock become lost in her? Despite his expertise with ropes and chains, was it possible—could she brand him with what was woman about her?

"Damn, damn, damn," she hissed. The last *damn* echoed.

He didn't dare fuck her after all, at least not with his cock. Safety—and he knew a great deal about the word—lay in dictating her responses, not the other way around. How could he have forgotten that!

Forget *intimacy*. He'd wear her down and force her to spend herself. Then when she was all but unconscious from his practiced handling, he'd tell her she could leave because he had no more need of her. He'd show—

"Kade, Kade?"

"What?"

"I want...I want this to be for you, too."

Chapter Five

Although Kade's fingers remained buried in her, he'd stopped moving them. In the energized silence, Maita sensed his disquiet. Instead of asking for an explanation, she held herself in readiness.

"For me?" he repeated.

"Yes." She clenched and relaxed her cunt muscles to demonstrate what she had in mind. "I've seen you at work, remember. The way you handled Lisa—it was rough but what she wanted. Everything you did was for your client, but I'm not one of them."

"No. You aren't."

He sounded unsure of himself, perhaps because he was trying to find her place in his life. That made two of them. "I want sex," she admitted. *Hell, I'm already being fucked.* "But you deserve the same."

"Why?"

Why? The question rocked her. "You're incredibly sexy and complex, a man who undoubtedly understands women more than they do themselves, who puts their needs and desires before his own." *Was she insane, carrying on a conversation at a time like this?* "You have to be frustrated. I want to change things for you."

His palm pressed against her opening, splintering her thoughts. "Why?"

"Be-because I care about you. You. Not just what I hope you'll do to and for me."

"Care?" he whispered. "You don't know what you're talking about, Maita. You can't possibly."

"Then tell me."

Instead, he pulled out of her, gripped her hips and pulled back and up, positioning her on her knees. Willing to accommodate him, she braced her upper body on her elbows and forearms. She even reached for her crotch and opened her pussy to him before he had to do the work himself. Finally, not sure she wanted to see him, she looked over her shoulder and up at him. He knelt between her legs, his arms hanging at his side, not touching her, not meeting her eyes.

"Do it. Fuck me in the way that works for you."

"This is for you."

"The hell it is! If you think I want to be taken like a dog the first time out of the chute for us— Do it, damn it!" Increasing her stance even more, she leaned back toward him and lowered her head again, increasing his access to her. "Get it on."

"Not yet."

She felt him move off the bed, heard a drawer open and then the unmistakable sound of a condom package being opened and put to use. He returned.

With a curse, he pulled her cheeks apart and drove into her. His strength and anger would have knocked her onto the bed if he hadn't clamped onto her rib cage and held her in place. Blood rushed to her head. She saw nothing of the man fucking her, felt only his cock rammed deep, his strong fingers keeping her where he wanted. Grunting rhythmically, he buried himself over and over again, the force keeping her in motion. Anger, frustration, even the thousand questions she had about this complex man became buried under the sensation of his engorged cock expanding her core.

He rode her hard and long, an expert cowboy controlling the creature under him. She felt like a bitch in heat. Her dangling breasts swayed in time with the pulsation. She became primal, an animal lost in her partner's power. Lack of control didn't matter. Neither did dignity. This man who'd laid claim to countless vaginas had chosen hers tonight.

Her scalp, cheeks, neck and throat became coated in sweat. They rocked and drove together, retreated, advanced over and over again. Her pussy walls caught fire. Wet friction spread over her, traveling up and down her body. He shifted his grip. His fingers ground into her skin as if trying to connect with the tip of his penis.

He owned her sex. She'd given up all claim to her body and turned it over to him to tease, punish, or treasure as he saw fit. In the total surrender she discovered hot desire. It spun an ever-expanding web and sucked her body and soul into it. She heard herself scream, then scream again. The raw sounds further fueled the flame.

She came and kept coming. Every muscle in her body seemed to have tightened. She couldn't find the *off* button so simply rode the climactic waves. Her scream went on and on, blocking out whatever sounds he made.

* * * * *

"You had sex with him, didn't you?"

Although she'd expected to start the day by talking to her boss about the schedule for the rest of the week, Maita said "yes" without giving away any emotion.

"After I told you not to."

"What I do on my own time is my business."

"The hell it is!" Rylan looked around, probably assuring himself that no one else was in the barn and might overhear. "You forget, I know how the bastard operates — the same way I've been known to do." He took her hand and turned it upward so he could stroke her callused palm. "You're far from a hothouse flower which has a great deal to do with why I hired you, but at the core of you is a woman. Sensual. Responsive."

Muttering a curse, she jerked free. "Whether I am or not is my business. I don't wear your brand. You don't own me."

"Don't tempt me."

The thought of becoming a man's possession caused her cunt to soften. A moment later reality intervened. She had no interest in having this particular man's rope over her. "I'm not trying to," she pointed out. "Do you want to let me in on what you want me to do today, or are you going to criticize my behavior?"

"Normally your behavior would be the last of my concerns as long as you do what I hired you for, but we're talking about Kade Severn."

Kade Severn. The name stroked her and brought back memories of climax and the aftermath when he'd watched, silent and naked, as she dressed and walked out of the room made for sex in its baser forms.

"Maita, I know what he's capable of." Rylan pinched the bridge of his nose. "Whatever skills I've gained when it comes to bondage is a result of watching him at work. He's the master. I'm the willing and happy pupil."

As long as Ann and whatever other women crossed Rylan's path were equally content, what did she care? "He's your teacher?"

"Because I insisted on it. It's a seductive lifestyle, Maita. And in Kade's hands, you don't stand a chance."

"Thanks for the warning," she said to cover a niggling unease.

"I can tell it'll take more than that to convince you you're making a dangerous mistake by letting Kade get his hooks into you. He'll change you then discard you. Speaking of hooks, how'd he play you?"

Not me, Lisa. "I'm not telling you anything."

"You don't have to. I can imagine."

Wonderful.

She'd started to reach for a bridle when Rylan grabbed her and forced her hands behind her. At the same time, he drove her back against a wall. "Listen to me and listen good! You're right. I can't dictate your actions when you aren't on the clock for me. But if you keep seeing Kade, he's going to suck you dry of everything except needing his brand of sex. You're a sensual woman, strong and alive, curious and natural. Perfect for him."

"I'm not paying—"

"Do you think that's what he gets off on? If you do, you're even more vulnerable than I thought. I'll tell you what. Ask him about his childhood. If he tells you, you'll know why he's so dangerous."

* * * * *

She'd fallen asleep on the blanket-covered couch in the cabin. Night had crept into the room, the only light came from the flickering TV she'd been watching before dozing off.

Her first awareness came when a floorboard creaked. Feeling drugged, she started to sit up. Strong hands twisted her onto her stomach, burying her face in the blanket. Fighting for breath distracted her from what the intruder was doing until it was too late. Once he'd lashed her hands behind her and roped her ankles, he turned her onto her side. She started to scream. The man clamped a hand over her mouth, then rammed a strip of leather between her teeth and fastened it behind her head.

Caught. His.

A knife made short work of her blouse and bra. Her jeans resisted attack so he unzipped them and slid them down as far as the ankle restraints allowed. Taking more rope, he secured her upper arms so her elbows nearly touched in back then finished his handwork by looping the rope both under and over her breasts.

*She now lay looking up at him, her head propped on the armrest. She still couldn't make out his features, and his manhandling hadn't told her anything about his identity. When he ran his hand under her panties, she tried to evade him, but the couch trapped her as surely as the ropes did. His fingers on her belly left bruises in places and in ways she couldn't escape. Along with fear came another equally unfightable emotion —
sexual excitement.*

She prayed he wouldn't discover her reaction, but he worked his fingers between her legs and treated himself to her hot juices, then wiped them on her erect nipples. After entertaining himself by playing with her unbelievably sensitive labia, he hauled her upright. He forced her toward the door, her mincing steps drawing out the leaving, but finally he had her outside. Then he threw her over his shoulder and carried her to a truck with the passenger's door open and ready to receive her.

"We're going to my place," he said. "I'll bring you back when I'm done with you — if I'm ever finished."

* * * * *

Maita stood behind the loading chutes watching a couple of hands force a big black mare into the cramped space. According to the experts, bareback riding was the rodeo's most physically demanding sport, but although she'd worked out for at least an hour every evening this week to prepare for the local rodeo, she couldn't keep her mind on what she'd be doing in a few minutes.

She hadn't seen or spoken to Kade all week. He'd been out of town taking his stock to a California rodeo but had gotten back the night before last. When he hadn't tried to contact her, she'd told herself she was relieved. After her vivid dream, she needed distance between herself and the fantasy it had conjured up. At the same time, she chafed at the idea of being a one-night stand to him. She'd been good enough to scratch his sexual itch, hadn't she!

But maybe—what did she mean maybe—some other woman was scratching him now.

How many women had been, were, and would be in his life? The questions kept her on edge. At the same time, she had no explanation for why the answers meant so much to her. After all, they'd only had sex once.

Once. It wasn't her place or right to ask him about his childhood. Or his to know about hers.

"I wasn't sure I'd see you here," Ann said as she threaded her way through the uniformly dressed men with their cowboy hats, tight jeans, and well-used boots. "The way you rode the other time, I thought you might be chasing the big time instead of opting for this podunk event. Of course," Ann leaned close and spoke into Maita's ear, "staying close to home increases the chance you'll see Kade."

"Is he here?" She tried to keep her voice casual.

"Who knows. Sometimes he hangs around to keep an eye on the stock he runs here. Sometimes he has other commitments."

"He's a busy man."

"Too damn busy." Obviously not concerned with Maita's need to physically and mentally prepare herself for her ride, Ann pulled her away from the chutes. "What was it like?"

"What was what like?" Maita asked although she suspected she already knew the answer.

"Boffing him. Or was it the other way around? Come on, give me a taste. I can still dream, can't I?"

"There isn't much to tell," she said, her attention on the arena where the clowns were entertaining the crowd between events. "Look, we'll talk later."

"Like hell there isn't! Don't forget, I've been under and over Kade. I know what he's capable of. Damn, do I." She made a show of pretending to wipe drool off her mouth. "Look, my man's waiting for me so I can't stay long." Ann stroked her crotch. "I've got a new piece of jewelry. Keeps my mind on sex full-time. Talk about a high! You should get Kade to install one on you."

"Not likely."

"Yeah, you're right. Having that man pulling your strings, so to speak, is asking for losing your sanity once and for all. Shit. It sure as hell happened to me." Ann shook her head. "Rylan said he tried to warn you off Kade. I'm not going to do the same. I just want you to be sure you know what you're doing."

"I'm about to compete in a riding event."

"Sure you are. The master's back in town. I can as good as see him zeroing in on you."

* * * * *

Damn it, I don't know what I'm doing, Maita admitted as she settled onto the black mare's back. The instant her crotch came in contact with bone, muscle, and hair, all thought of Kade evaporated. She became what she both loved and feared being, a bareback rider. Her personal rigging had been strapped around the mare's belly, and she now slipped her gloved hand into the handhold. Not satisfied to simply wrap her fingers around her only way of staying on the black's back, she pounded on her glove until the leather conformed to the well-rosined loop.

Balance, rhythm, control, she kept chanting. With her free hand, she pushed her hat firmly in place and lifted her legs so her boots would be over the point of the horse's shoulders when the mare's front legs first hit the ground out of the chute.

She felt calm, nervous, focused.

"Ready?" the chute master asked.

She sucked in a breath and lifted her free arm. "Ready." She dropped her arm.

Daylight! Movement! The gate was still opening when the mare exploded. Maita concentrated on raking her dull spurs down the mare's shoulders in a *good lick*. The instant she'd completed the motion, she fought to bring her legs back up so she could repeat the required movements. The judges stood on either side of the chute, watching her technique and judging the mare's action.

Buck! Kick! Lunge! Hit the ground like you're a pile driver! she encouraged her mount. *Change direction. Twist and roll!*

Perhaps hearing her, the mare flung her hind legs upward. Because Maita's back all but kissed the horse's rump, the hind legs came dangerously close to striking her head. An instant later, the bronc catapulted herself into the air and came down hard on her close-bunched legs. Maita bit her tongue. Her brain felt shaken.

Keep your damn arm up. Whatever you do, don't touch –

Halfway through her mental reminder not to do anything that would disqualify her, she felt the horse spin to the right. Thrown off balance, she fought to return to an upright position. The arm all but welded to the animal felt as if it was being torn out of its socket. Try as she might, she couldn't retain enough control over her body to continue spurring. She'd managed to lift her legs and start a downward movement when the mare suddenly raced toward the end of the corral. At the last instant, she stopped, front legs outstretched, haunch dragging on the ground.

Maita kept going.

She had a splintered vision of herself being launched over the horse's head, fingers stripped from its hold, sailing almost gracefully. Then she struck the wooden fencing and slid to the ground.

Ignoring the clowns headed toward the small unmoving figure, Kade galloped to where Maita had landed. He catapulted himself off his still-running horse and knelt before Maita. Her eyes had rolled back, one leg was twisted behind her. She lay partly on her back, arms askew. Experienced in handling injured cowboys, he placed his hands on either side of her head to stabilize it and waited for her to breathe.

"We'll take care—" one of the clowns started. "Severn? What are you doing here?"

I don't know. "Why not?" he snapped. "I'm riding pick-up tonight anyway."

The clown nodded and turned his attention to Maita. To Kade's relief, her eyes fluttered open. She blinked repeatedly.

"Don't move," he ordered when she started to straighten her leg. "You don't know where you're hurt."

"Kade?"

"Good guess," he quipped to hide his concern. "Stay like you are. Where do you hurt?"

"Where don't I hurt?" She started to laugh, then winced. "Boy, I blew that dismount, didn't I?"

"How about your head? You were knocked out."

"It isn't the first time." A serious expression settled in her features, making him wonder if she was assessing her body.

"Can you move your legs?" he asked.

"I'd better. Until I get out of here, the rodeo can't go on." She straightened her leg and brought her hands up to her face. "All systems working. I want to sit up."

Want? As in accepting my help? Despite his concerns about her neck and spine, he ran his hands under her shoulders and helped her into an upright position because the alternative meant holding her down. A struggle could cause more damage.

"Shit!" she gasped.

"What! What's wrong?"

"I'm going to look like the victim of a beating by morning." She ran her hand over the back of her neck. "As soon as I can figure which direction is up, I'm out of here."

Instinct—or something—took over. Without asking permission, which he suspected she'd deny him, he gathered her in his arms and stood. He fully expected her to demand to be let down. Instead, she rested her head on his shoulder and wrapped her arms around his neck. The trusting gesture touched him in ways he couldn't comprehend. She stayed like that as a clown put her hat back on. Then they left the arena accompanied by applause.

"That's right, ladies and gentlemen," the announcer said over the clapping. "Let the little lady know we're rooting for her. And for those new to our little rodeo, her hero is none other than Kade Severn, owner of the stock being used here. From the looks of things, this particular cowgirl has already forgiven him for supplying her with a bronc capable of launching her like something from a slingshot."

After slipping through a gate, Kade headed toward the small trailer he'd hauled to the county grounds so he could spend the night with his stock. Maita felt small, warm, slight, and vulnerable in his arms. For someone accustomed to carrying women where he wanted in preparation for doing whatever he wanted, he felt strangely out of his element. This time, this woman, hadn't hired him to test her capacity for bondage and everything that went with it. Neither was she someone he'd picked up at a bar. She was—what?

Because he'd locked the trailer door, he had to put her down so he could pull the key out of his pocket. In the distance, the crowd shouted encouragement to the next rider. Moths and other insects attracted by the overhead mercury lighting flew around them. The air smelled of animals and hay. And the woman he'd been thinking about since the day he'd first seen her stood beside him.

Although he wanted to pick her up again, he needed to watch the way she took the two narrow aluminum steps into the trailer. She attacked them slow and measured but sure. After unlocking the door and opening it, he joined her in the cramped space and turned on the light.

When she removed her hat, he saw she had a lump on her right temple, her outfit was covered with dust. Other than that, she looked none the worst for wear. Why then couldn't he stop mentally replaying her accident and feeling this gut-level fear?

"Sit down," he ordered. "I'll get you something to drink."

"Water, please. And aspirin if you have it."

He filled her request while she sat on the single bed that doubled as a couch. After washing down the aspirin, she stared up at him. "You don't usually do pick-up, do you? More important things to deal with, right?"

"Usually, yes."

"But tonight was different, why?"

Because I knew you'd be riding. "It's a good thing I was out there. Otherwise, you would have had to exit under your own steam."

"Which I'm perfectly capable of doing." She fingered her swollen temple. "I look like shit, don't I?"

You look incredible, strong and feminine all rolled into one. "Why do you do it?" he demanded. "What the hell are you trying to prove? Do you have any idea how few women try bareback?"

93

"I don't need to *prove* anything. I've always stood on my own two feet."

"Always? What about when you were a child?"

She laughed, the sound harsh. "Where do you think the training began? My childhood serves as a model for the term throwaway kid."

On the verge of asking if she hurt somewhere beside her head, his thoughts hung up on her unexpected admission. "You were abandoned?"

She stared which made him wonder whether she'd surprised herself by her candor. "For lack of a better term, but I'm over it...or I guess you could say I learned how to adapt. Look, I don't want to get into my history tonight. I'm not sure I ever do." She closed her eyes, breathed deeply then opened them. "I appreciate you carrying me here and giving me drugs. Thank you. I'm not used to needing or accepting help."

Just like me.

"But you need to get back to work and I might as well go home since I'm sure not in much shape for celebrating afterward...if I even had something to celebrate."

He fully expected her legs to go out from under her, after all, that's what happened in the movies when the script called for a romantic scene. However, although she had to lean against the wall, she remained standing. The trailer was so small he could barely turn around when just he was in it, and yet he felt distance between them. She held herself apart from him, a loner who didn't know how to rely on anyone.

"It doesn't have to be like this," he said.

"What doesn't?"

"You. Making it on your own. Thinking you always have to do it all yourself."

"It's what I want."

Her words were simple, yet complex, a summation he both understood and felt a stranger to. The women he worked with all wanted something from him—not emotionally but physically. Either they were determined to explore their own sexuality or were preparing themselves to accommodate some man's demands and desires.

In marked contrast, all Maita needed from him were a couple of aspirin.

"Kade," she said softly, her hand on the doorknob. "It might not make sense to you, but I like my life the way it is. I don't have any experience in relying on another human being."

She'd opened the door and started out before he spoke. "What will it take to change you?"

"Too late."

Chapter Six

"What are you afraid of?"

"Nothing. You want me to get back on your worthless old nag, just name the time and place."

"I'm not talking about bronc riding, Maita."

Kade's challenge hung in the air. His hard glare didn't help. He'd called the morning after the rodeo to ask how she was doing. Although it had taken all she had to get out of bed, she'd told him she was fine, thank you very much. Maybe he'd read something in her voice that gave away the lie and maybe his story about wanting to see Rylan and having planned to come out this way anyway had been the truth. Either way, when he'd shown up three days ago, she had been out at the barn preparing to work with another barrel horse.

She'd chatted briefly with both men before hoisting herself into the saddle and riding off for the area set up for practice. To her consternation, they'd wandered out her way and watched for a while. By the time they'd left, her jaw ached from clenching her teeth to hide her aches and pains, and her head throbbed.

Kade had dropped by unannounced the next day to let her know he was taking delivery on a half dozen new Brahmas and did she want to come see them. This time he'd caught her trying to put on a bridle with her left hand because she couldn't lift her wrenched right arm above shoulder height. He hadn't had the good grace to pretend not to notice but had demanded to know why she insisted on pushing herself. She'd snapped that she wasn't about to play invalid.

Fortunately she hadn't seen him for a couple of days, but here he was again standing in her doorway throwing accusations at her. Even worse, his faded jeans fit so damn tight his bulge left little to the imagination. He smelled of aftershave.

"Then what are you talking about?" she demanded although she'd have preferred any other topic.

"Rylan didn't know you'd been knocked out. Why the hell didn't you tell him?"

"I can still do my job." She lifted both arms over her head and turned from side to side demonstrating her now returned flexibility. "He doesn't care about anything else."

"The hell he doesn't, and you know it. Damn it, why won't you let anyone get close?"

I don't know how. "You and I fucked. If that isn't close, what is?"

"But it only happened once."

She wasn't about to tell him about erotic dreams and midnight masturbation. Neither could she imagine admitting how much she wanted to throw herself at him at this very moment, to acknowledge his understanding of her and beg him to master her.

No! To present herself to him for the taking represented the height of vulnerability.

"Maybe I was waiting for an invitation," she quipped.

"Speaking of invitations, are you going to ask me in?"

"No."

"Why not?"

"No one else is around, in case you didn't notice. I need to work, not argue with you."

"You're throwing up barriers."

Look who's talking.

"I'm not one of your bimbos, Kade. You can't lay claim to me."

He stepped toward her, and it took all she had to stand her ground. When he caressed her still-tender temple, she told herself he was demonstrating normal curiosity. Then he pressed his hand against the back of her neck and forced her toward him, and she had no rationale for either his action or her reaction.

"You fascinate me," he said. "I keep wondering what it would take to break you down and have you begging for what I can give you."

At his words, her teeth all but floated. The strength went out of her, and her arms hung at her side. A lifetime of having total responsibility for herself, body and soul, evaporated. Turning herself over to someone else for manipulation, for the very breath in her lungs was terrifying and exciting at the same time.

"I can't afford you." Her voice sounded weak.

He kept the pressure on her neck. "I'm not charging."

"Who says I'm interested?"

"You won't know until you try—unless you're afraid."

Afraid! No.

Propelled by the challenge, she twisted away. She half expected him to come after her, but he remained in the doorway—filling it and affording her no escape.

"Go away!" she ordered. "I don't want—"

"Yes. You do."

* * * * *

Maita rode bareback. The gelding showed promise as a jumper and although she'd told her boss she'd work with the horse while he was gone, instead of practicing pacing and placement, she'd taken him out for a long, easy run. Sitting on his sharp backbone hadn't accomplished much except to keep her on edge sexually, but at least the ladder of spine had given her something to rub herself against.

Feeling more frustrated than she'd been when she'd hoisted herself onto the gelding, she headed home. She should clean out the barn. True, she'd wind up hot and dirty, but at least she'd be too tired to care about anything except a shower. Maybe.

She halted the gelding at the entrance to the barn, dismounted, and walked him into his stall. After unbridling him, she filled his water bucket and made sure he had enough hay. It was definitely cooler in here, and she was loath to move.

However, she wouldn't sleep tonight if she didn't get more exercise.

With the reminder propelling her, she rubbed the gelding's forehead and shut the gate behind him. She started toward the barn entrance.

A half dozen steps from freedom, someone grabbed her from behind, pinned her arms against her sides, and pulled her off her feet. She started to kick back. Before she could land a blow, the intruder threw her facedown into a pile of hay. Barely able to breathe, she fought to get her arms under her, but they sank into the hay. A large male straddled her waist, his weight pinning her hips. She felt rope circle first one elbow and then the other. Then her captor yanked her elbows together behind her back and quickly tied them. Her wrists were still free, but what did it matter?

She concentrated on keeping her head turned to the side so she could breathe. The man quickly, expertly, turned around and repositioned himself so he now faced her legs. Once more she tried to kick but as with her arms, he easily snaked more loops of rope around her ankles and tied them together. Although she wore boots, her feet were useless. Her lungs burned with the desire to scream, but the ranch complex was deserted. No one would hear her.

The man again lifted himself off her. He planted one hand between her shoulder blades and pressed down, and worked her shirt out of her waistband. He pushed the shirt up as far as her belly-down position allowed.

She knew those hands.

"Kade? Damn it, what—"

Before she could finish, he grabbed her braid and pulled her head back. She felt something being pressed against her teeth forcing her to open her mouth. The moment she did, Kade gagged her with what felt like a short length of wooden dowel. Next, he released her hair and hooked something—maybe leather—behind her head, which kept the dowel in place. She could still utter a muffled sound but what was the point?

Although her nerves felt about to explode, she didn't resist as he rolled her onto her back. He was dressed in black, the short-sleeved pullover shirt clinging to his muscled chest and arms.

"You're going to learn a lesson today," he told her. "When I'm done with you, we'll see if you feel the same way about turning yourself over to someone else, giving up control." He pushed her shirt up over her breasts then worked her bra upward freeing her breasts. "You fear not being in charge of your body. I don't blame you. I don't." He stroked her breasts. "But it's time for you to change...and to experience the pleasure of surrender."

The pleasure of surrender? No! she told him with her eyes, but he didn't listen. Instead, he pulled her to her feet and threw her over his shoulder. She might have managed to dislodge herself if she fought, but she'd still be his prisoner.

To her shock, he walked over to and into Rylan's house.

"In case you're curious," Kade said, "your boss usually locks his door, but he knew I wanted to use a certain room."

What room? She lifted her head as best she could as Kade took them down a hall she'd never been into. She thought he might go into the bedroom she assumed Rylan shared with Ann. Instead, when he stood her upright, she found herself looking down a set of stairs.

"I don't want to take a chance on falling so you're going to walk," he informed her. "And in order for you to navigate the stairs, you'll need your feet."

It took him only a moment to untie her ankles. He kept his hands on her, stroking her calves, thighs, and then hips as he straightened. He closed his hand around the elbow restraints and pushed her to the top of the stairs. "We'll go down together."

He'd taken her into a basement. Even with the lights off, she had no doubt where they were because the room had the musky smell she associated with below ground spaces. He'd closed and locked the door at the top of the stairs. Because she had no idea what the room contained, when he let go of her, she didn't take a step. Although she was tuned in to her surroundings, she didn't know he'd returned until he snagged her wrists and tied them together. The double arm bonds forced her to arch her back. She didn't want to think about what her exposed breasts looked like, especially with the bra pushing down on them.

Why didn't he turn on the light?

He unsnapped her jeans and pulled them and her panties down over her hips. The fabric now around her knees tethered her.

"Slow," he muttered. "Slow and steady. Bit by bit I'll change you. Introduce you to what your body's truly capable of."

She didn't want to be here! Wanted back daylight and freedom! At the same time, his words held promise.

This time when he lifted her off her feet, it was to deposit her on what had to be a mattress on the floor. He'd positioned her so her upper body rested on her bound arms, and she lay there like an about-to-be-branded calf while he removed her boots, socks, jeans, and finally her panties.

She expected his hands on her crotch but was still waiting for the touch when he looped rope around her ankles, crossing one leg slightly over the other. More rope soon circled her just above her knees and sealed her pussy closed. Then while she waited to see what he would do next, he unbuttoned her blouse and reached behind to unhook her bra. While she wondered how he'd remove the rest of her clothes, he rolled her onto her belly and untied first her elbows and then her wrists.

She could have fought, scratched and struggled. Instead, she mentally and emotionally went with his hands as he undressed her. Then he retied her wrists behind her and positioned her on her side. A mental image of him kneeling over her weakened her and sent her thoughts, her response to her sex.

Helpless. At his mercy.

He was doing something to her wrists, but she didn't try to make sense of it until he pulled up on her ankle restraints so her legs were bent. Demonstrating more of his expertise, he tied her ankles and wrists together.

She felt him get off the mattress. A few seconds later he switched on a light. Once her eyes had made the adjustment, she saw she indeed was in a basement although dungeon better described it. The stone and timber walls sported several metal rings fastened to them. Other rings hung from the ceiling or had been embedded into the stone floor. She spotted a cage in one corner, its dimensions so small whoever was placed in it could hardly move. As for the other *furniture*, she didn't want to think about their uses.

"Now you know your employer's other side." Kade stood over her. "As long as Ann entertains his fantasies, she'll be the only one—other than you today—to come in here, but Rylan gets restless. And as you can see by the decorations—" He swept his arm over the room. "He needs variety."

Variety? Was that why Kade had *kidnapped* her, because he'd grown bored with what he usually did to women? But why her?

"You're hogtied," he said. He continued to stand, forcing her to look up at him. "The line of a naked woman with her back arched, her breasts ready for whatever I want to do to them, and her limbs useless is beautiful. I might take pictures so you know what I'm looking at."

Helpless.

She thought she'd buried the word years ago, but when he knelt beside her and placed his hands over her breasts, it surged back to life. She tried to shrink away from him but only managed to press herself another inch into the mattress.

"I could play with you like this for hours." He worked his fingers against her flesh, sending friction to her nipples. "Bring you to the brink and then back you down—over and over again. Think about it, Maita." He transferred a hand to her hip. "You're a calf. I'm the cowboy who has just lassoed you."

He caught her right nipple between thumb and forefinger and rolled it back and forth. As he did, he worked his other hand between her legs and pressed against her. "I'm going to brand you but not in ways you've ever seen. You can't move, can't fight. There's no one watching this event, no judges telling me to release my calf. If I wanted, I could drag you from one end of the arena to the other."

What are you doing? she tried to ask with her eyes. His threat, if that's what it was, should have terrified her. Instead, sexual excitement touched her nerve endings.

He maneuvered a finger inside her. "Wet. I thought so. Being helpless turns you on, doesn't it?"

When she didn't respond, he lightly slapped first one breast and then the other. She tried to squirm away which earned her even harder slaps. Furious, scared and turned on all at the same time, she redoubled her pathetic efforts at fighting. Her struggles earned her another finger up her cunt coupled with his callused hand now pressing so hard on a breast she felt weighted down.

"I love doing this," he informed her. "And I'm damn good at it. I know how the game is played and constantly make up new rules, new moves. By the time I'm done with you tonight, you'll never be the same. Your priorities will have changed."

Priorities?

Still pressing on a breast, he began a stroking motion along her labia that nearly duplicated the feel of a man's cock. Although she wasn't cold, she began shivering, all thoughts of resistance faded. Yes, he knew what she needed. Yes, his methods were crude and frightening. True, she hated both of them for what was taking place, but laced in with self-disgust, release began. Each stroke brought her closer to welcome relief. He controlled more than the existence, time, and tempo of her climax. Her body no longer belonged to her—he'd demonstrated his greater power and knowledge. In gratitude and surrender, she turned herself over to him.

"Feel it," he ordered. His finger-fucking quickened and hardened until she rocked to his tune. "Become part of my gift to you."

He leaned over her, cupped the base of her breast and pushed it up. The firm drawing sensation took her attention from his other manipulations. She couldn't find the line between pleasure and pain. Then he closed his mouth over her captured breast, pressed his tongue against her taut nipple, and sucked. At the same time, he withdrew from her cunt, settled his hand onto her mons and began stroking her clit. Her roped legs made resistance impossible, and her strength went into fighting her trembling, and handing herself to him.

She felt his work-roughened finger pad on her clit, teasing, testing her boundaries. Her belly clenched. Hungry, she arched herself toward him and threw back her head.

My body. Belonging to you. Your prize. Your possession.

Her pussy muscles began a familiar clenching and release. He'd left her opening empty, but she could climax without being fucked. She would because he demanded it. Behind the gag, she moaned.

"No. Not yet."

Brought back to reality by cool air on her wet and sensitive breast, she blinked repeatedly. He'd straightened but kept his finger on her clit, which made it nearly impossible for her to concentrate. Fire danced, but although it licked at her, he kept her from jumping into the flame.

"I'm not letting you climax so quickly. First you need to understand more about my power."

What more is there? I'm your prisoner.

But a prisoner was someone who had been thrown behind bars because she'd broken a law or maybe was a political pawn, not a modern, law-abiding woman. If he'd left her with the power of speech, she'd demand clarification.

Or not.

He climbed off the mattress. Maybe she could have rolled onto her other side to see what he was doing, but what was the point? He'd only place her where he wanted her when he returned.

Waiting, she became aware of the strain in her shoulders and the saliva soaking her wooden gag. Her thighs ached, and she longed to be able to straighten her legs. Most of all she felt throbbing need between her legs.

He'd promised her a climax. But when and in what form?

"Still here, are you?" he said from behind her. "Well, of course you are. I want to fuck you, Maita. More than you can imagine and more than I— But if we have sex again, it levels the playing field."

And he didn't want that? Could he be afraid of seeing her as his equal?

She told herself the thought was ridiculous, but even as she waited for his next move, she couldn't dismiss the question. After what seemed like a long time, he stroked her temple.

"You're a beautiful woman," he muttered. "Independent and courageous. Insane."

Insane?

"You fascinate me. I can't stop thinking about you. I want to see and touch and fuck you." Although she'd already tested her gag's effectiveness, he did so by tugging on the straps and checking the positioning of what was in her mouth. "I want to bring you pleasure. Although I think the time would come when you asked me to use my skills on you, I've decided to call the shots. I don't usually care because as long as I'm paid, what the hell does it matter."

He'd stopped touching her face. Tense again, she strained to discover what he had in mind for next. To her shock, he slipped a cloth over her eyes. Instinct kicked in, and she fought to see again, but of course like every other round, he won this one.

"You can't speak and now you can't see," he pointed out unnecessarily. "Sensory deprivation makes most women docile. Given your *bring on the world* attitude, I'm not sure you'll react the same way, but I want to find out."

To her relief, he loosened the tension between her wrists and ankles, then removed the rope near her knees. Next he lifted a leg, demonstrating his improved access to her sex. Lost in darkness, she imagined him staring at her while he savored his mastery. She'd never mentally placed herself in such a submissive position.

"You don't know what I'm going to do to you," he said. She thought he was standing near her head but couldn't be sure. "You can anticipate—or fear, depending on your mindset. But the only thing you can do is wait. Wait and wonder what your master has in mind."

Master? Never!

She hadn't finished the thought when he again separated her legs as much as the ankle restraints allowed. Although it did no good, she couldn't stop from trying to see. She'd just resigned herself to more waiting when she felt something hard being pressed against her pussy. She struggled to scoot away.

"Not going to happen, my pet. I've just begun to play."

The object began to vibrate. Caught in emotions she couldn't name, she tried to relax, but although she managed to stop struggling, her pussy muscles resisted all attempts to control their reaction. Slow, so slow she thought she'd die with the waiting, he increased the vibrator's power. Her body shook and shuddered under the assault. She sucked in a breath and held it, felt heat dance through her pelvis. Her already hard clit tightened which made it even more susceptible to the sensual attack.

He no longer needed to force her legs apart. She did that for him — for herself. Her breathing became so loud it grated on her nerves. At the same time, the ragged sound added to her reaction. The vibrator had a hard round head with a small but equally hard knob at the tip which Kade put to mind-blowing use by pressing it against her clit.

How he kept it in contact with the small, all-feeling, juice-soaked organ was beyond her. Her cunt flowed. Fluid seeped out of her and told him everything.

Sensation rippled up from her tortured clit to encompass her pelvis, belly, and breasts. She longed to curl around the sex toy, but because he'd robbed her of movement, she could only turn herself over to it — and to him. She now breathed in grunts. Head thrown back in an attempt to reach for enough air, she struggled to give him even greater access. The battery-run sex toys she'd used on herself had been like nags left in a trained thoroughbred's wake. She rode this stallion, this ruler of all things sexual, climbed and sweated, sobbed and strained for the summit.

Then, again, he denied her.

Chapter Seven

"Do I have your attention?"

Maita hadn't tried to move on her own since Kade had removed the blindfold and untied her except to turn her head to see if he had an erection. The telltale bulge reassured her that he was human, but she couldn't say where his humanity began and ended.

"Yes," she said when he removed her gag. She lay limp and hungry and unsatisfied on the mattress and waited for her master's next move. "You have my attention."

"I thought so. So, are you ready to redefine your definition of control?" He sat on the edge of the bed, positioned her on her back, and straightened her legs. Was this his way of saying he had no more interest in her sexuality?

"Redefine?" she repeated. If she begged—*begged*—would he fuck her? Did she dare ask?

"I'm guessing it didn't take as much to strip you of everything you believed about self-determination as you thought it would. One touch with this—" He indicated what she now saw was a black vibrator run by electricity. "And all bets are off, aren't they?"

"What's your point?" she demanded, her nude body within his easy reach.

He frowned, and his hands turned into fists. When he unselfconsciously stroked his crotch, she imagined him naked with his cock poised over her hungry opening. "I'm giving you proof," he said, "of what else your body is capable of."

"Else?"

He scooted closer before closing his thumbs and forefingers over her hard nipples. "Besides risking your life on the back of some damn animal."

He played with her breasts for several minutes while she dug her nails into the sheet and remained accessible to him. "What do you want?" he abruptly asked. "I can do whatever I decide, but I'm curious. If I give you an option." He indicated the room with its myriad of instruments and equipment. "You're going to get played with, but you can pick your poison so to speak."

She should jump to her feet, kick him in the balls, and run for freedom.

But he'd only overtake and overpower her. Or let her go.

"A climax."

* * * * *

Maita stood near the middle of the room. A few minutes ago, Kade had positioned her with her legs widespread and then tied her ankles to floor rings so she couldn't change position. Next he'd placed heavy metal cuffs on her wrists and fastened chains to the cuffs. The chains had hung from an overhead pulley so she wasn't surprised when he engaged the pulley and pulled her arms over her head. The strain in her shoulders distracted her from what he was doing with the result that he'd already locked the metal collar around her neck before she truly felt it. Like the handcuffs, he added chain to the collar. Instead of being attached to an overhead pulley however, this restraint led to the wall behind her. He wordlessly tightened the chain which pulled her head back. She couldn't move.

"You can still speak and see," he pointed out needlessly. "I want you to think about what's been done to you so far and anticipate what I have in mind for next."

Why? she wanted to know but suspected he didn't have an answer—for either of them. Besides, she didn't want to distract him from what she hoped would become release from the awful sexual tension still knotted around and inside her.

She'd seen him use a whip on another woman, but she shuddered when he ran the silken strands across her body. She wasn't a paying customer hungry for pain. She was…what?

"So you need a climax, do you?" he taunted as the slaps increased in intensity. "Don't like the way I brought you to the edge and left you hanging, did you?"

"No!"

"But I decided it was necessary because it taught a lesson about mastery—my mastery."

He changed focus, now lightly whipping her exposed crotch. Each blow, if she could call them that, sent a shudder through her. Once again her pussy heated. She should hate and fear pain! Instead—

"Let your imagination grow," he said in a deep, somber tone she hadn't heard before. His words were in rhythm with the mild punishment. "You're no longer a modern and ambitious woman. You're chattel, possessed by a man with the right and strength to do whatever he wants with you." He ran the whip over her exposed throat. "You live or die depending on his whim."

"No," she whispered.

"Yes. But you don't fear the future because as long as you satisfy his needs, he'll bring you pleasure. You live in a nearly constant state of arousal." Proving his point, he ran his hand over her crotch and deposited her wet offering on her inner thigh. "Whatever you need to do to get him to give you release, you'll do it."

He moved behind her and began swatting her ass with the whip. Although she had to concentrate on breathing, she couldn't ignore the fire he'd set off inside her. She burned, the flame beyond her ability to extinguish or control.

"But your master doesn't easily or often grant release. He knows you'll remain receptive to his control as long as he has your full attention." She heard the whip land on the floor. "Your world narrows down until everything revolves around sex." Proving his point, he spread her ass cheeks and ran his fingers over her rear opening. "You don't care. Nothing else matters."

"You're wrong." She'd hoped to sound strong. Instead her protest came out a whimper. "I'm not chattel."

He released her cheeks. She heard him moving about and waited, alive and desperate. When he touched her again, he began by rubbing something she suspected was body oil over her ass. He deposited more of the warm oil inside her butt and demonstrated its effectiveness by slipping his finger a couple of inches into her rear opening.

"Have you ever taken a man in the ass?" he asked.

"No!" Her throat closed down, forcing her to whisper. "He has no right."

"Past tense, Maita. Past tense."

No, no, no. The chant filled her ears. But even as she silently protested, her nipples hardened in anticipation. She tried not to let her pussy muscles clench, but they'd escaped her control.

He fastened something around her hips that made her think of a garter belt except it also had cords or wires that hung down in front and back. With her head forced back so she couldn't see anything except the ceiling, she could only imagine. He offered not a single word of explanation as he pressed something against her ass. *A butt plug!*

Scared and excited, she did her best to relax while he slowly worked it into place. The device now filled her. Consumed her. She thought it might slide out when he stopped pushing on it, then realized the plug was attached to whatever he'd placed around her hips. When he was satisfied with his handiwork, he held up something that looked like a TV remote for her to see.

"Ten speeds," he told her. "Probably more variation than you'll give a damn about, but I wanted the best quality." He pushed a button on the remote. The plug came to life, the buzzing barely noticeable. Still, she twitched in her bonds. He pushed again. This time she felt movement throughout her butt hole.

"What— Please!"

"Please what, Maita?"

Another level of electrical charge briefly distracted her from the question. "Why are you doing this?"

She expected him to say *because I can.* Instead, he gently stroked the side of her neck. "I've never met a woman like you," he whispered. "I can't get you out of my mind." He continued stroking her as the plug moved and challenged inside her. "I'm making sure it'll be the same for you," he said and stepped away.

Why? By turning her head as far to the right as possible, she saw him settle into a cross-legged position on the floor. He began rubbing himself.

"Ready?" he asked. Before she could so much as think about a response, the plug's vibrations became so intense it claimed her full attention. If she screamed *I can't take it!* would he release her from this torment?

Only, it wasn't torment. Sensation licked over her. True, her ass had become the center, but waves radiated out to kiss and tantalize her throat, breasts, pelvis, thighs. She imagined her pussy lips turning red, her clit swelling. Moisture dribbled out of her opening to coat her inner thighs. The strain in her arms and legs added to the sensation. She'd become, what, a cunt? Maybe. A hot and hungry cunt.

"Do me, do me, do me," she chanted. She didn't know or care what she meant by do. He rewarded and punished her by driving yet more power into the plug. It now felt as if it had found its way into her vagina. As it licked at hot, sensitive walls, curled upward toward her mons and from there to her belly.

She rocked in the prison he'd created for and of her. She heard nothing beyond her own noisy breathing and the occasional senseless plea forced from her.

Climax? No, not yet. Just a little more electricity, perhaps another swat from the whip. But fascinated as she was by what her body was capable of, most of all she wanted to be wrapped in his arms with his cock housed in her.

For them to be equals.

"How close, Maita?" he asked. "When you're ready to come, let me know."

"I need…more."

Maybe he'd kicked the plug up another notch. She couldn't tell. Beyond anything except needing release, she closed her eyes. In her mind, no longer was she restrained by bonds. Instead she'd willingly, gladly assumed this position because it brought them both pleasure. He enjoyed manipulating her response so she'd placed the plug in herself and handed the operating device to him. She heard her voice directing him to increase the vibrations, and he told her what watching her did to him sexually. They became partners in stimulation, kindred souls with the same goal.

Close! Muscles tightening over and over again. Nipples feeling like rocks and her clit throbbing.

"Coming!" she wrenched out. "Oh god, coming!"

She felt the plug rocking on top speed, pain-pleasure in her captured limbs, her throat stretched, her pussy—

Him! His hand on her sex, teasing and promising, fingers in and out, in and out, pressure against her lips and clit, her mons being rubbed.

"Mine," he said.

Then waves caught her and nothing else existed.

* * * * *

Kade had removed the plug and released Maita's legs and neck, but he'd kept her wrists restrained and the now loose ceiling chain attached to the cuffs. She sat on the cold floor, her hands near her pussy, legs slightly bent. She stared unabashedly at her herself and repeatedly licked her lips.

"Thirsty?" he asked.

"Yes, please."

Leaving her, he went into the small bathroom for a glass, but instead of returning to her, he stared at his reflection in the mirror. His eyes had darkened, something he'd long associated with sexual excitement. His cock felt as if a clamp had been attached to it, and he'd left marks in his palms from clenching his fists.

"Bastard," he told the unexpectedly old-looking man staring back at him. "What the hell are you trying to prove?"

Although he fought it, the image of Maita lying unconscious in a rodeo arena rose in his mind. He'd seen downed cowboys before and had experienced enough injuries of his own. One more victim shouldn't have this reaction on him.

But it had because this time…

Unnerved by the remote possibility that he'd been about to admit he was falling in love with Maita, he switched off the light and stepped back into what Rylan delighted in calling his dungeon.

Maita hadn't moved. Locks of hair had come undone from the thick braid and obscured much of her features. The whip had left faint marks on her stomach and legs, and her neck looked red from the collar. Rope marks circled her ankles.

She was his. She belonged to him. If he wanted, she'd spend weeks and maybe months naked with his restraints on her.

Once again the sense that he was out of control washed over him. In the past, once he'd finished with a woman, he wanted her gone and out of his life. He knew his reaction was his way of emotionally separating himself from someone who'd exposed everything of a sexual nature about herself to him. He'd never tell the women this, but once they'd degraded themselves—or rather he'd turned them into something primitive—he'd felt a measure of disgust for both giver and receiver of climaxes.

Today he studied Maita and thought of a superb horsewoman long accustomed to living life alone and on its own terms. He admired her. That was it! He admired her—surely nothing else.

Although her movements were awkward, she took the glass and drank deeply. When she was done, she indicated she wanted him to sit next to her. Not sure why, he did so.

"I want to tell you how I feel about what happened," she said. "But I can't sort things out yet. Maybe after I've had time to think—" She tried to rotate her wrists in the restraints. "I haven't felt anything like this for so long," she whispered. "I thought I'd put it behind me."

He picked up the chain and used it to draw her toward him. As he did, he studied her expression. She had the familiar spent look of a woman thoroughly fucked, but he also recognized intelligence returning.

"So long? What did you think you'd put behind you?" he asked although he sensed he shouldn't.

While he gripped the chain hard enough to cause his fingers to cramp, Maita explained that her father had been killed in a motorcycle accident when she was five. She lived with her mother for a couple of years after, mostly in a series of trailers where she pretended to be asleep while her mother made her living by spreading her legs. Then her mother had been arrested for something, maybe theft but maybe drug dealing, and while she was in jail awaiting trial, a man who said he was Maita's uncle had gotten custody of the child. For a couple of weeks, Maita had thought of little except how wonderful it was to have a full-sized bedroom and silence at night.

Then the uncle had rented and filled a moving truck, told Maita to climb into the passenger's seat, and started driving. They were on the road for days, sleeping at rest stops and eating at fast food restaurants. He'd finally pulled up at a derelict house near the outskirts of what she eventually learned was Dallas. The house didn't have air conditioning or a yard and apparently the school system didn't know about her because she didn't remember going for several years.

"I don't think he was my uncle," Maita said in an unemotional tone. "I might have been nine when he got custody of me—if he really did. We didn't stay in Dallas long. Every few months we'd pack up and move again."

"Weren't you a burden to him?" he asked although he knew the answer.

She shook her head. "I became a valuable commodity. I earned him a lot of money."

"He turned you into a prostitute?" He had to force the question.

"No." She'd been staring at the floor. When she looked at him, he found remnants of the helpless child she'd once been. "There's a lot of money in child porn, Kade. My uncle became good at exploiting me, damn good. I try not to think about that time and what I was forced to do, so don't ask. As I got older, I became less valuable to him in that department. Fortunately, by then I had a pretty good idea what would come next. That's when I ran away."

"Did you have him arrested?"

"No." She sounded surprised that he'd asked.

"Why not?" Anger against a man he'd probably never see knotted his muscles. What he did was one thing—considered reprehensible by all except the consulting adults involved—but to exploit a child took someone unworthy of the term *human being*.

"It wouldn't have changed what happened," she told him. "Believe me, I wanted him to pay for what he did to me, and if I'd thought there was the slightest chance he'd do it to another girl, I would have run to the police."

"How can you be sure he's cleaned up his so-called act? A leopard doesn't change his spot."

"This one did." She clenched and unclenched her fingers. "He's in prison—for income tax evasion and identity theft."

"White-collar crime," he said as he picked up the key and released her hands. "I'm surprised they didn't give him a slap."

Not taking her gaze off him, she began massaging her wrists. "I attended the trial. I'd sit in the back of the courtroom, saying nothing but with my eyes on him the whole time. I learned I could scare him. The feeling was incredible! To finally have a semblance of power over him— He'd made the mistake of trying to steal a judge's credit cards."

Kade laughed and took Maita in his arms. "How long did he get?"

"Ten years. He's only been in three."

"Did hearing the sentence give you a sense of closure?" he asked although the last thing he wanted to do was pull her any further into the past.

"In a way." She laid her head on his shoulder in a gesture of trust—and maybe something else he didn't remember ever having been on the receiving end of. "But I'd gone on with my life. He couldn't touch me anymore. I didn't want to care anything about him."

He embraced her while her words worked their way inside him. The rest of the world no longer existed. There was only the two of them and the revelation she'd just handed him. "Is that how you survived having to do what he wanted?" he asked, because he needed to peel away yet more of her layers until, maybe, he found her beating heart. "You disassociated yourself from what was being done to your body?"

"I, ah, I hadn't thought of that."

"Did you?" he repeated and increased his hold on her.

"I must have. Kade, you don't want to hear about this."

"Yeah, I do. And you need to talk about it."

"Maybe," she said on the tail of a sigh. He ran a hand over her naked thigh, but she gave no indication she'd noticed. "When he posed me... When he made me do certain things, I'd pretend I was somewhere else."

"Where?"

"On horseback. Riding with the wind."

"Fantasy kept you sane."

"Maybe it did. No matter what was happening to my body, in my mind I'd be on that horse—the fastest and strongest in the world. I'd cling to his back and urge him on until his hooves no longer touched the ground. We flew. I'd feel his strength and heart and those things would become mine."

He held her at arm's length so he could again look into her eyes. "And did you do the same thing just now?"

She started to nod, then shook her head. "I think I could have if I wanted to, but I didn't try."

"Why not?"

"Because it was different with you."

Chapter Eight

Maita took a shower in the bathroom off Rylan's master bedroom and slipped into a short white terrycloth robe she suspected belonged to Ann. After towel-drying her hair, she followed her nose into the living room where Kade was scrambling eggs. As they ate, he told her he'd be gone most of the coming week because of a Canadian rodeo. If possible he preferred to get to the grounds a day before the rodeo was set to begin, both so his horses, bulls, and calves could rest up from the trip and because that gave SPCA officials time to inspect his animals. No, he said in response to her question, he'd never been fined by any agency charged with protecting animal welfare.

Although she'd seen enough of his stock to know he took good care of them, she hung on his every word. The contrast between the *slave master* role he assumed when it was called for and his dedication to animal welfare intrigued her. How could a man who willingly gave up sleep to care for a lame horse switch on another personality?

The simple answer was that dominating women gave him a sexual thrill and probably made him rich.

Only, she knew there was more to it. What eluded her was the why.

"Are you going to be home tonight?" she asked as she cleaned up after them.

"I think so. Why?"

"Alone?"

After a short pause, he nodded.

"I'll be there after dark," she said. She followed up her promise by giving him a peck on the cheek. Then before things got out of hand, she went down into the dungeon for her clothes.

* * * * *

Not bothering to knock, Maita turned the knob and stepped into Kade's ranch house. Even before she'd closed the door behind her, the smell of leather and wood touched her senses. No one was in the living room so she stood in the night-dark room and listened. She caught a faint hum of voices and followed the sound down a short hallway. Even before she reached the room with light streaming from the cracked door, she realized the voices came from a talk radio program.

She pushed the door open a few more inches and looked in. Kade sat at a massive desk that held a laptop, fax machine, and several stacks of paper. He was writing and stopping occasionally to sip from a bottle of beer. He'd taken off his shoes but otherwise looked dressed for a day of physical labor.

He'd told her the truth. He had no woman in here tonight.

"Are you going to come in?" he asked without turning from his work.

"You heard me?"

"Maybe. I just *knew* you were here." He wrote for a couple of seconds, then swiveled his chair around to face her.

She'd thought she'd be ready for the sight of him. The lamp on the edge of the desk was bright enough that his rough edges showed. He wasn't a handsome man. The elements hadn't been kind to him.

"I'd like to ask you something," she said. She'd thought her voice might give away her unexpected nervousness, but it sounded the same—calm and direct. Because she wore an oversized T-shirt, she wasn't sure he could tell she hadn't bothered with a bra. If not, he'd soon find out.

"What?" He stood but instead of coming closer, he leaned against his desk.

"Do you ever allow the tables to be turned? Has a woman ever tied you up?"

"No. Never!"

"Why not?"

"Because I don't want it."

"Want? Or are you afraid of being helpless?"

He clenched his jaw, his eyes narrowed. "What is this about?"

She'd seen this defensive stance in a wild horse. Despite the rope around its neck, the animal refused to back down. "I thought you might want to put yourself in one of your *subjects'* positions. It could be a way of improving on your technique."

"Are you complaining? You want to go another round, see if I can up the ante?"

Not tonight. I'm still finding me. "You're avoiding my question, Kade. You really don't have any interest in letting a woman take charge?"

"None."

His response had come quick and had been hard-edged. Once again she was struck with the nagging feeling that he was throwing up barriers. "All right," she said and shrugged as if no longer interested in the subject. "Unless I get a lot stronger, there won't be any reverse role-playing. I'm not going to be able to subdue you and throw you over my shoulder, am I?"

"What's this about?"

Good question. Instead of putting voice to what had brought her there tonight, she unceremoniously pulled her top over her head and exposed the breasts he'd already touched and tasted and owned.

"Earlier today was about me," she informed him. "Tonight is going to be about you—what I can do for you."

"Why?"

Why? The question probed deep. "It's what I want to do," she said. "Can't we leave it at that?"

No, his eyes said.

"What are you afraid of, Kade?" she challenged.

"Nothing."

Liar. "Maybe. Maybe not. Tell me something. When's the last time a woman pursued you instead of the other way around?"

"What the hell are you getting at?"

"You've erected a wall around yourself, don't try to deny it. As long as you call the shots, you convince yourself it's the way you want your relationship with women to be. But what if someone—me—refused to play according to your rules?"

He took on a wary, wild animal look, but although she might have been able to force her way past his defenses, she didn't try. Being alone with him reminded her of what she needed from him—and what she'd vowed to do for him.

"I'm sorry," she said and slid nearer. "I should know the ground rules, shouldn't I?" A few more steps brought her so close he could have touched her if he wanted. His clenched fists told her how much self-control it took to keep his hands off her.

"The first time I found myself in a corral with a horse, nothing mattered except getting on his back and riding." She tugged on his western-style shirt. After freeing it from his jeans, she ran her hands under the hem and pressed her fingertips against his waist. "I wasn't afraid. Fear never entered my mind."

"Then you were a fool."

"So I've been told. But even when I'm thrown, I have no qualms about doing it again." For the better part of a minute, she didn't try to organize her thoughts. Instead, she concentrated on memorizing the feel of him and learning her reactions to his heated flesh. "Being thrown has taught me to do everything I can to anticipate when and how and under what conditions a horse is going to buck. I've also learned how to hit the ground."

"Unless you've been knocked out."

"True," she acknowledged and smiled. He didn't. Wondering what was behind his somber expression, she unbuttoned his shirt and without fanfare pulled it off him.

"You're beautiful," she told him with her palms pressing against his nipples. "I know. A man doesn't want to hear he's beautiful, but you are. You're made for what you do—both with animals and women." Although she hadn't had enough of the feel of his hard nubs, she slid her hands down his sides, demonstrating the lack of extra flesh. "If I was to design the perfect man, I wouldn't change a thing."

"What about the scars?"

"I have enough of my own. They prove we're alive."

"There are many kinds of scars, Maita. Not all are on the surface."

"If you're talking about my so-called childhood, I'm well aware of the impact it left on me." Standing on tiptoe, she kissed him. When he didn't respond, she settled onto the balls of her feet and studied him. "It took a long time, a hell a lot of lonely horseback rides, but I finally convinced myself I wouldn't let that bastard rule the rest of my life. What he'd done to me was in the past. I was going forward."

"And you have." It wasn't a question.

"Where are you?" she asked. "What are you thinking about?"

"You're an incredible woman," he muttered after a too-long silence. "There isn't a thing you're afraid to tackle, is there?"

Hadn't he already said that? And had her approach to life really been on his mind? "I don't know. What kind of *thing* did you have in mind?"

"What I did to you didn't frighten you."

"I'm not sure," she admitted. "You brought out reactions I never thought possible, ones I had no control over. Wonderful as the climaxes were, they also unnerved me." She indicated his desk. "Did I interrupt something?"

"Nothing I didn't want to be interrupted from. I'm expecting a phone call. Other than that—" He finished by running his hands behind her and pressing lightly on her shoulder blades.

She hoped he'd say he was at her disposal for the rest of the night, but when he didn't, she reconciled herself to the message behind his silence. He wasn't a man who turned himself over to any woman. He kept his core under wraps.

Could she change that? Did she want to?

"I love the smell of your place," she told him. She hooked her hands around his waistband and tugged him toward her. To her relief and delight, he came willingly. "Masculine."

"No argument there."

Fingers still inside the waistband, she entertained both of them by rubbing her knuckles against his belly. Soon, soon, she'd have access to all of him—and he to her. "Did you decorate it yourself?" she asked. "Maybe you had help."

"If you mean was a woman involved in choosing the furniture and other stuff, no."

"Why not?"

His fingers stilled. When she looked up, she saw he was frowning. "I knew what I wanted. Besides, there was no woman I wanted to consult with."

No woman important enough to have input in creating this sanctuary? Unnerved by the question of where she stood in the scheme of his life, she briefly struggled with the possible answers and then shoved it all aside. "Well, you've done an awesome job," she said as she worked his snap loose. "Everything about it says this is the home of a man's man."

"A man's man?" He pulled her against him which trapped her hands between them and left her without enough freedom of movement to tackle his zipper. "Is that how you see me?"

"I'd never try to put a label on you, Kade. And I hope you haven't done that with me."

"No. I haven't."

The three words held depth and mystery, but as long as his cock pressed against her, she couldn't concentrate on them. His half-erection brought her back to the reason for her visit. Although she loved feeling him from breast to belly, she strained against his arms. His grip slackened, but he kept his hands on her waist. Putting her mind back on her plan, she dispensed with the zipper and slid his jeans down over his hips. She left them clinging to his thighs and turned her attention and fingers to his cock. A moment later she slipped it through the opening in his shorts.

His cock looked disembodied, separate from the rest of him, an organ designed for only one thing.

Her legs felt weak. Instead of fighting her reaction, she sank to her knees in front of him. As she did, he ran his fingers into her hair which she'd left free, but didn't try to stop her. She wanted to put her mouth around him, but the pleasure could wait while she fulfilled other fantasies.

She began by blowing on her palms until they became damp and warm. Then she made a steeple of her hands over his cock. His cock was too large for her to enclose its length, not that she minded. Once she'd lubricated him with her moisture, she slipped her fingers to the side of his shaft, exposing the head between her thumbs and forefingers. Inch by slow inch, she worked her palms down his shaft and pressed just enough to provide a measure of friction. He'd become fully erect by the time she reached his scrotum. His hold on her hair tightened.

"I'm not going to hurt you, Kade," she whispered. She'd placed her mouth so close that her breath reached his tip. "I'd never hurt you."

"Don't...make a promise...you can't keep."

Casting aside a niggling unease, she moved her fingers back up his length, careful to keep him housed. His grip shifted to her shoulders, maybe so he could pull her off him if he wanted. His quickened breath and taut muscles left no doubt of his reaction.

"Sit down," she said.

"What?"

"Please, sit down."

After a moment, he positioned himself over his office chair. Before he could lower himself onto it, she released his penis and pulled both his jeans and shorts down around his knees. Looking less than in control for the first time since she'd met him, he placed his naked ass on the seat. After rocking back on her heels, she lifted one of his legs at a time and stripped him. Her mouth felt dry. In contrast, she'd already soaked her panties' crotch. Much as she longed to tighten her buttocks, she struggled to keep the focus on him—on bringing him pleasure.

First she lubricated his cock by sucking him into her mouth and covering it with saliva. She reluctantly released him but immediately took him into her hands again. This time she positioned her fingers on either side of his shaft and held him upright. Applying light pressure, she stroked every inch of taut flesh. She occasionally brought his cock toward her and closed her lips over his tip but kept the contact brief and teasing.

By now he was leaning back in the chair, legs widespread, hands gripping the armrest. He rocked from side to side, but she didn't loosen her grip. Despite her determination to put him first, she clenched and released her pelvis to deal with her excitement.

"Can't..." he gasped, "take much more."

"Yes, you can."

He again took hold of her shoulders, his grip bordered on the painful. In it she sensed his reluctance to let a woman dictate the course of their sexual encounter, but so far he hadn't tried to stop her.

What did she mean, try? If he wanted, he could have her on her back and spread-eagled in a matter of seconds.

Her imagination kicked into high gear. Even as she stroked and teased by lightly running her nails over his engorged veins, she lost herself in fantasy... *Her attempt to give him head hadn't pleased him. Determined to teach her a lesson, he yanked her hands off him and threw her facedown on a bed. She made a show of struggling, but of course he won the battle. Exhausted, she didn't resist as he ordered her to bend her knees so her ass stuck up in the air, legs spread as wide as she could get them. Then he expertly demonstrated the art of tongue play.*

"Slide forward," she ordered in a strangled tone. "Spread your legs."

"Damn it, Maita. I—"

"Forward." Despite her lightheadedness, she tugged on his cock. "Now."

To her relief, he scooted toward her until his ass was half off the edge of the chair. In this position, he could no longer hold on to her and was forced to grip the arms to keep from sliding off. Feeling as if she'd managed to run a Brahma into a corral, she set her mind to drawing out the lesson. A wild animal fought any and all ropes placed on it, but if the trainer went about things slow and calm, at length the animal understood who was in charge.

She began by taking hold of Kade's cock and drawing it up so she could see its underside. His legs looked so taut she wondered how long he could hold his position, maybe no longer than she could resist straddling him and easing him into her.

Fucking. Pure and simple sex.

Soon. Soon.

Holding his organ up and away from him gave her access to his scrotum, yet she hesitated touching his family jewels. Life's promise lived within the twin sacs. He held more than sperm in there, more than fluid she hoped would soon fill her. If she wasn't on the pill and he didn't use rubbers, he might impregnate her. She'd carry and then bear his child. No matter what happened between the two of them, they'd always have something precious in common.

Did she want his child?

Did she want her world changed? To no longer be alone?

Incapable of answering the questions, she lifted his cock even more. If he asked, she'd have to admit she didn't know what she was doing when she pressed her palm against the silken flesh under his balls. The moment she did, he arched off the chair.

"Maita!"

She continued to press. He remained poised on the edge of the chair, head back and breathing loud. Her naked breasts ached to be touched, and she regretted not having removed her jeans, but maybe it was better this way. Her sex remained out of reach.

Giving in to desire, she stroked his perineum using small circular motions with her thumb pad. Her focus remained on the organ cradled in her other hand, its promise, vulnerability, and potential.

"The whole time you were turning my body into what you wanted, I thought about doing the same to you," she admitted. "I'm not like you. I'm no expert. But, I think, if I was a man, this is what I'd want."

She changed to an up and down motion. Traveling no more than a half inch with each stroke, she imagined her fingers inside him. The thought of burying her fingers in his anus stole her breath. Would he allow her to rule him in such a way? Could she make herself stop?

He suddenly tensed even more. "Your...nails."

"I won't hurt you." She continued stroking. "I'd never—"

The phone rang. She continued to hold him. It rang again. "I have—" he started.

"Answer it."

Although she kept her fingers against the flesh under his balls, he started to straighten and reached for the instrument. His "What?" sounded terse and distracted.

"No, not this weekend," he said after a moment. "Weekends aren't convenient for me."

They weren't because his rodeo business went into high gear then. Weekdays were better for...his other occupation. Feeling a little sick, she stopped trying to distract him but kept her fingers on him.

"I don't need the money, Sam. I don't give a damn if you triple it." He listened. "I'll get back to you." Another pause. "Fine. Think about it. When you've made up your mind, let me know." He hung up without saying goodbye. "If it rings again, I'm not answering."

"This Sam wants you to, what, *train* some woman?"

"Sam's a middleman." He sounded reluctant to speak. "I've gotten a lot of work because of him."

Work hardly explained Kade's service. "What do you want him to make up his mind about?"

"Whether he'll use me again." He leaned forward, took hold of her wrists, and drew her hands off his cock. "I'm sure he knew I was otherwise occupied."

"And if he doesn't ask for your...your services again?"

"He will. He's trying to play hardball, but I hold the bargaining chips." After glancing down at his engorged organ, he gave her a sidewise glance. "I thought, if she doesn't stop playing with me, I'm going to come so damn loud I'll burst Sam's eardrums."

"I didn't want to stop," she admitted, "but I thought the call might be important."

"It wasn't."

* * * * *

Kade lay on his back on his bed, his eyes never leaving Maita as she slowly circled him. Following his admission that he could care less about Sam's offer, she'd asked where his bedroom was. He'd surprised himself by leading the way. Then she'd *ordered* him to present himself for servicing, and he'd complied.

She'd more than taken her own sweet time getting rid of the rest of her clothes and killed even more time reaching inside herself for proof of her sexual excitement. As she made her way around his bed, he wondered if he'd tell her he'd never before brought a woman into this room.

Brought? No, she'd called the shots tonight, not him.

Coming smack up against the reality of his solitary bedroom distracted him from what he hoped to hell was about to happen. He'd had access to countless women over the years. It made sense to work them in his specially designed room. As for those he'd chosen to have sex with... Hell, it wasn't as if this rural part of the country was overrun with single and willing women. Fortunately, the rodeo atmosphere had proven to be more than conducive to one-night stands.

One-night stands? Not always. Sometimes he spent the entire time he was in a town with the same woman.

But he'd always kissed her goodbye and driven down the road.

"This is my way of saying thank you," Maita said as she crawled onto the bed. She positioned herself near his feet but didn't touch him.

"For what? Multiple orgasms?"

"No." She placed his feet on her thighs and began massaging his insteps. "I don't know if I've ever told anyone so much about my upbringing. I guess...maybe having you physically and sexually expose me freed me."

"I'm glad." He meant it.

"Do your other, ah, women unload the way I did?"

The others weren't mine. I simply provided a service. "We didn't do a lot of talking."

"Then I'm the only blabbermouth?"

The mix of pressure and gentle strokes on his feet distracted him from a great deal—or maybe he wasn't ready to face what she'd brought up. Soon, damn soon, they'd fuck. In the meantime, he'd turn certain parts of his anatomy over to her, not to further sexually stimulate what was ready to rock and roll, but because, because...

Peace and relaxation seeped out from her fingers, traveled up his legs, heated his pelvis and belly and of course his cock. Sensation radiated out until he felt her touch on the top of his head and tip of his fingers. The greatest heat settled around his heart. His pulse quickened and nothing beyond this room—this woman, mattered.

Once she'd been a scared and helpless child exploited by a monster. Somehow she'd survived and now faced life with courage and strength. He had no doubt that somewhere deep inside her lived remnants of the girl she'd once been, but he'd seen her reckless courage and gentle, caring nature around horses. The monster who'd exploited her hadn't destroyed her humanity.

Her honesty touched him as no woman ever had.

The moment the thought hit, he forced it away. Without knowing, she helped by shifting her manipulations to his calves. As she kneaded away the knots deposited by a long, physical day, he embraced the calm, warm world she'd created for him. He surrounded himself with it, barely existing.

She began humming. Because his bedroom windows were open, insect sounds blended with her barely audible notes. His eyes closed. He found himself in a universe of clouds and endless prairie. Out here civilization and responsibility couldn't reach him. Alone in this place he loved, he simply was.

Then she spread his legs, climbed into the space she'd created and used her magical fingers to locate and minister to the knots in his thighs. Consciousness returned. Whenever she wanted, she could take hold of his cock and…and what, command him?

Maybe. She understood him, at least she did his sexual nature. She had the power to turn him into what she wanted him to be, just as he'd manipulated countless women.

Opening his eyes, he locked his attention on her and told himself that at least she hadn't found the way to his soul.

Then she returned his gaze, and he was no longer sure.

Or if he wanted to keep his own past hidden from her.

Chapter Nine

A few moments ago Kade had looked so peaceful Maita had been content to work his leg muscles. When he closed his eyes, she wondered if he might fall asleep, but his penis had served as proof of his conscious state.

Then he'd looked at her, and she'd returned the connection and known something had shifted in him.

Instead of asking for an explanation she didn't believe he'd give her, she forced her questions aside.

"I'm not a masseuse," she admitted as she straddled his legs. "I figured you must have been on your feet most of the day and would appreciate a little TLC."

"I did. I've never had—"

"You haven't?" Although it put strain in her back and caused her breasts to sag, she leaned down to place a kiss on the tip of his cock. "All right, here's the plan. At least I think I have this worked out. We could waste time on foreplay, but I'd prefer to get to the main event." She kissed him again, this time drawing out the contact. He dug his nails into the coverlet. "From the looks of things, you're ready. So am I." Feeling no embarrassment, she lubricated her fingers with her juices and deposited it on his shaft. His knuckles turned white.

"Not yet." He sounded as if he was strangling. "First, a rubber."

"I'm not ovulating."

"I never fuck without one."

Because you don't trust the women to tell you the truth? "What if I said I was on the pill? Would it make a difference?"

"No. They aren't perfect." With something between a groan and a curse, he lifted her off him, got to his feet and half stumbled over to a dresser. He pulled out a box of condoms and slipped one in place. Then he returned and positioned himself as he'd been before.

As he watched unblinking, she settled herself so her vagina was directly over his cock. The moment the organs made feathering contact, she reached down and guided him into her. Much as she wanted to swallow him *now*, she took him slow, savoring his heated length and breadth.

His hardness softened her and pulled her thoughts and emotions off everything except the act of fucking. Once she was sure he'd begun the journey to her core, she released him. Head back and hands on her hips, she savored. Her thighs felt hot, her pussy swollen and hungry at the same time.

"Where...are you?" he asked.

"Nowhere. Feeling."

Gripping her pelvis, he buried himself deeper, fuller. She acknowledged his mastery in such matters. The moment went beyond gratitude for an experienced sex partner and touched on the trust she innately felt—trust that allowed her to lay herself bare to him.

She'd think about this later. Now—

Suddenly he pulled her down onto him. Keeping the connection between their sex organs intact, he rolled onto his side. Now she lay beside him, her body cradled in his larger one. Not looking at her, he began pumping. At first his thrusts threatened to knock her back. Then, finding a small measure of logic, she braced herself on her elbow and hip. Bending her knees made it possible for her to ride and rock with him, to prepare herself for each assault. She stared at the blur of his chest, her knees occasionally scraping his thighs.

They didn't quite fit—the size difference was too great for a seamless union. But his cock glided over her lips, against her inner walls, repeatedly kissed her clit, and she didn't care about anything else.

The room smelled of man and the world beyond the open window. Her flesh caught fire, flames that blended with his, became part of him.

He increased his pace. His muscles turned to iron, and he evolved into a pulsing machine. Although she grew dizzy from matching him thrust for thrust, she raced up the mountain with him. She felt the first hot explosion of semen fill the condom. Then her cunt muscles spasmed, and she cried out her delight.

Together! Climaxing as one!

* * * * *

When she heard the knock on her door, Maita's first thought was that Kade had come to see her, but he'd told her he had to go look at a couple of possible saddle broncs and wouldn't be back until tomorrow night at the latest. As for whether he'd want to get together when he returned or had other business to tend to—

Shaking off unwanted images of him plying his *trade*, she opened the door to find herself face to face with a weeping Ann.

"Can-can I come in?" Ann managed.

"Of course. My god, what's wrong?"

Ann didn't say anything until she'd collapsed on the couch that went with the cabin. "Do you have a drink?"

Maita poured a Coke and whiskey for both of them and sat on the opposite end of the couch. "Give," she ordered after Ann had taken a big swallow. "What the hell's going on?"

Ann downed more whiskey. "I need— Will you do a favor for me?"

"What is it?"

After yet another swallow, Ann removed her shoes. Then she stood and pulled off her jeans. The black panties came next. "This." Ann fingered the tiny clit ring. "I need fucking help getting rid of it."

"Why don't you want it?"

"Because he doesn't want me!" Ann slumped onto the couch again. She rested her head on the back of the couch and slid forward, exposing her clean-shaven cunt. "I thought...the trip we've been on... I thought he wanted us to have a vacation together." She wiped her nose on her shirttail, prompting Maita to hurry into the bathroom for a box of tissues.

After loudly blowing her nose, Ann continued. The first night at the luxury hotel in southern California had been everything she could want complete with hours of sex and sex play on a heart-shaped bed with an overhead mirror. "Then the next night he took me to a club."

"What kind of club?" Not staring at Ann's sex was hard.

"I don't know what the hell it was called, but I sure as hell know what it exists for—trolling."

"A meat market?"

Ann shrugged and fingered her ring, then shuddered. "Big-time meat market. All right, you want the whole damn story? It's used for BDSM. Masters putting their slaves up for bid. Would-be buyers sampling the wares."

Wonderful! "Rylan sold you?"

"They're negotiating." Ann finished her drink and blew her nose again. The whiskey must have hit bottom because she stopped crying. "When the man—I don't even know his name—paid to play with me, I didn't object because I figured Rylan was priming his pump, getting us both ready for an even better time together."

Not more than an hour ago, Rylan had called to say he wanted to talk to her. She'd assumed it was work-related and had agreed to drop by his place before going to the barn in the morning. Now she didn't want to have anything to do with him. Yes, Ann was a fool for allowing herself to become Rylan's sex slave, but how could he have dismissed her this way, if that's what he'd done.

"Did you go with the man?"

"Yeah." Ann shuddered. "I need another drink."

She left Ann to contemplate her pierced clit while she mixed another drink. Ann straightened long enough to dispense with half of the fresh whiskey, then slumped and splayed herself again.

"My new *master* hates this." She fingered the ring. "He told me to get rid of it before I come to him."

"Are you going to?"

"What choice do I have?"

"Choice! Damn it, Ann, you're free, white, and twenty-one. You don't belong to any man."

"You don't understand! I love being pampered and manhandled. Being a sub means I don't have to scrape up a living. I get all the sex I could possibly want and beyond. Some...some is pretty rough, but the trade-off is worth it."

"Then why are you crying?"

Ann blinked and stared. "I don't know. Shit, yeah I do. I thought Rylan loved me. When he places me naked in a cage and makes me stay there all day, I spend the time thinking about him, waiting for him to return. He knows...*he knows* I'd die if he left me like that. Doesn't my goddamned trust mean anything to him!"

"If you died, he'd be charged with murder."

"I gave him everything, held back nothing. Some of the things he made me do were pretty damn degrading and submissive. Just try to get some other bitch to— Doesn't he understand he owned my heart?"

Your body, yes. But if you gave him your heart, you're a fool. "What happens now?" she asked because she'd heard all she wanted to of Rylan and Ann's version of undying affection.

"I wait." Ann stared at the ceiling then closed her eyes which left Maita with damn little beside labia to look at. "Rylan said... He said I still belonged to him until the money changes hands, and he expects me to—"

"I got it."

"Yeah, I suspect you do. After all, you and Kade swing the same way."

Instead of objecting, Maita bit her tongue. A few seconds later, Ann went on. "He's going to expect me to show up at the dungeon tonight. Did you know he has one?"

"I've seen it."

"Has he—"

"No!"

"Hmm. Anyway, I know the drill. When he steps into the room, I'd better be ready and willing or he'll make it even rougher on me." Ann licked her lips. This time when she touched her clit ring, her hand stayed there. "I'm always scared...scared and so excited I spend the day before masturbating. By the time he starts in on me, I'm so primed... But it's going to be different tonight." She sniffed. "He's done with me, ready to move on, looking for new conquests."

"Then get out of there." Before, Ann had fascinated her. Now the other woman's submissive nature disgusted and depressed her. "Pack up and head on down the road. You have money of your own, don't you?"

"Money? I haven't needed any for a long time. Rylan..." She slid her middle finger into her cunt and started stroking herself.

"Stop it! I'm not going to sit here and watch you play with yourself. If that's what you came for—"

"No!" Ann sat upright and wiped her hand on her hip. "I'm sorry. It's just that I'm so damn fucked up. Maita, please help me get rid of the ring! That'll show him."

* * * * *

Not sure what she was thinking, Maita swung into the saddle and took off down the road on one of the barrel racing horses she'd been working with. Her boss expected to see her in a little bit, but if she didn't get a handle on her emotions, she'd be lucky if she didn't get herself fired.

Fired? Could she continue working with Rylan?

Before long, she realized she'd guided the mare in the direction of Kade's property. He was still out of town, at least he'd told her he'd be. She could revisit the scene of…of what? The crime? And maybe get her head on straight.

At least Ann had stopped crying by the time the small tin snips she'd brought with her had done their job. Maita had had to grit her teeth before slipping the instrument around Ann's clit ring. Even then she'd had to wait a few more seconds until Ann stopped shaking. Fortunately, the thin gold was easy to sever, and she'd used an equally small pair of pliers to straighten the ring and slip it off Ann's clit. She'd be a liar if she didn't admit touching Ann so intimately hadn't been a turn-on, and Ann's lingering kiss had held more than gratitude.

"I feel free!" Ann had exclaimed as she held the proof of her former slavery. "Wow, I just had an idea. What if my new master wants to make use of the hole that's already there? I love diamonds. Do you think—"

Maita had distracted her by ordering Ann into the bathroom where she kept a bottle of anti-bacterial soap. When Ann returned, she'd talked her into getting dressed, then insisted she have something to eat to counter the alcohol in her system before leaving. Ann had been grinning and whistling as she drove off, an exuberant child looking forward to a new adventure.

Was that how people like Ann and Rylan looked at what they did? What about Kade?

Although she knew she'd eventually have to face the question, Maita shoved it aside as she neared the field where the Brahmas stayed when not on the road. From a distance, the massive creatures looked docile, differentiated from countless beef cattle only by their larger size and the humps on their backs. Up close, they proved to be more impressive but still not frightening, no surprise since they were so accustomed to humans that they usually ignored them. Things changed when they were forced into small chutes and some reckless human being sat on their backs. Then they turned into monsters.

She positioned the mare next to the solid wooden fence and watched the bulls as they either grazed or slept. In many respects, Kade was a Brahma. Given the right circumstances, he changed from professional stock contractor into master of women's bodies and minds. The layers of civilization—for lack of a better word—fell away then, revealing someone fierce and powerful.

Memories of his wild nature heated her throat and the hollow between her breasts. Seeking to quiet the energy between her legs, she pressed down on the saddle and rubbed back and forth. The mare sighed and tried to lower her head so she could eat.

"No." Maita tugged on the reins. The gesture mirrored Kade's command of her and further fueled her imagination. Staring at the bulls, in her mind she became a cow brought here to be serviced by one of the massive creatures. Her owner had decided to let nature take its course so had simply put her in an enclosure with the bull of his choosing.

Although she was in heat with hormones driving her response and reaction, the bull's domineering nature frightened her. As the father of her yet-to-be conceived calf approached, she backed away. But there was no freedom! He kept after her until he'd cornered her. No matter which way she turned, he anticipated, coming closer and closer. His massive cock hung nearly to the ground, and he smelled of sex.

Still scared but trapped, resigned, and driven by the instinct to breed, she turned her back to the bull and raised her tail.

No! She wasn't some damn stupid animal!

* * * * *

Rylan let her in and indicated they could sit in the living room. Despite her best efforts, Maita couldn't dismiss what was underground here. Had he already chosen Ann's replacement? Was he anticipating the new woman's introduction to the dungeon?

"Ann said you were the one who helped her rid herself of a certain item," he said after offering her a beer which she refused. "Knowing my little girl as I do, I have no doubt you've heard her side of the story."

My little girl! "I thought I was here to discuss business."

"We'll get there." Rylan took his own sweet time appraising her. Apparently she lived up to his standards because a smile played at the corner of his mouth, and his eyes darkened. She wasn't about to check his cock's condition. "But a long time ago, I learned that putting pleasure before work whenever possible keeps me healthy — and happy."

"And you happy comes before anything else?"

His smile faded. "Let me make something straight, Maita. You're a rare talent when it comes to horses. I'd be the first to acknowledge that. But my success in the business world doesn't depend on having you work for me."

"Is that a threat?"

"Just a statement of fact. I like your directness—almost as much as I do your potential." He shifted his gaze to her breasts.

They sat across from each other which meant he couldn't catch her by surprise if he decided to, what? "Why don't you lay it all out so we're speaking the same language."

Eyes glittering, he shook his head. "Your mouth is going to get you in trouble. I might put up with your smart-ass attitude, but he won't. He likes his women silent—unless he's making them scream."

With an effort, she clamped down on her anger. "I don't want to talk about Kade."

"Too bad because we're going to." He leaned forward, his hands resting on the insides of his thighs. "Ann thinks I've grown bored with her which, I imagine, is true. But if you hadn't come along—if I wasn't aware of your *education* at Kade's hands—I'd probably still be content with her. You're new territory, a new challenge. A prime specimen green broke at the hands of a master."

Green broke referred to a horse that has been introduced to man's domination but just barely. Damn it, she was hardly that! "I doubt you know that much about my relationship with Kade. You're just assuming." She took a steadying breath and decided to go for broke. "Besides, what do you want with someone else's woman?"

"Kade Severn will never have his woman. It goes against everything in his nature." Rylan settled back but didn't take his eyes off her. Maybe he thought she might bolt—or try to. "That's why I warned him off you at first. I didn't want you doing anything stupid like falling in love with him."

Love? Hardly.

"Let's get back to the subject at hand, shall we. I compensated Ann more than handsomely for *performing* for me. But she's a hothouse flower, a toy. She uses her body, not her brain. You're different, not just in the body business because yours is killer, strong and honed for action. You also have a brain. I've seen it in operation." His fingers slid closer to his crotch and drew her reluctant attention to his erection. "The combination of sex and intellect..." He shook his head. "I'm willing to pay plenty to watch them in action."

"And if I'm not willing?" She made as if to stand.

Once more his eyes glittered, reminding her of cold obsidian. "Then our association is over. Maita, I know a few things about green breaking myself. Why do you think I started by praising your horsemanship? Think of my flattery as a few sugar cubes before I throw a rope over your neck. You've had your sugar. I don't need a bronc that can't be trained to my saddle and made to stay in my barn."

Chapter Ten

Kade punched send on his cell phone and rolled up the window to cut down on the road and wind sounds. Behind his three-quarter ton pickup, the stock trailer rattled. The two-day-old orphan bull calf which shared the cab with him lifted its head off his lap.

"What do you want?" he said into the phone by way of greeting.

"Top of the day to you, too," Rylan responded. "From your tone, what'd you think I was, a bill collector?"

"Your name came up on the screen. What's going on?"

"Not much. Where are you?"

He told Rylan he expected to be home in a little over an hour then fought with thoughts of how he wanted to celebrate his homecoming.

"Good," Rylan said. "We need to talk."

"What about?" *If something's happened to Maita —*

"I'm in the market for a new toy. Ann bores me."

"Maybe you bore her."

"Fuck you. She's getting a decent severance pay, and I've already lined up her next master. In the meantime, I've got no one to play with — so far."

"What do you mean, so far?" he asked, an uneasy feeling gnawing at his gut. The calf, worn-out from learning to drink from a bottle, dozed off again.

"I think you've got my point. Let me ask you a question. You got any hooks in Maita or is she up for grabs?"

"Stay away from her, damn it!"

His outburst earned him the laugh he'd expected. As long as he lived, he'd never fully understand Rylan. The man seemed to be split into equal parts. He admired the savvy businessman who'd turned his parents' hard-scrabble ranch into a successful horse breeding and training operation, he couldn't say the same for the bastard who'd spent years leaping from woman to woman.

At first Rylan had been like most well-heeled single men, effortlessly drawing beautiful women to his money. But for reasons Kade didn't understand and didn't particularly want to, Rylan was no longer satisfied with *normal* relationships. Maybe it was a power play on his part, maybe it took BDSM to get a rise out of his cock. *It's different for me. It is!*

"Kade, old buddy, I want you to think back on something," Rylan said. "When you first latched eyes on the broad under discussion, I told you to leave her the hell alone. Are you trying to turn the tables?"

"I'm saying she's not some animal you've decided to hunt."

"What the hell do you call what you're doing?"

Before he could think of a response, Rylan continued. "I gave her a choice. You know me, always the diplomat." He laughed. "She can either play in my playground—oops, dungeon—or she can find herself another job."

Despite fantasies of smashing his fist into Rylan's face, Kade kept his voice calm. "You're going to fire the best trainer you've had unless she plays your sick game?"

Rylan snorted. "Look who's calling it a sick game? You're the one who gets the players ready, who teaches them the rules. The reason I called, *good buddy*, is because I wanted to consult on something. I'm not going to fight you over ownership of Maita. If you've already branded her, say the word, and I'll put you to work finding me a new pet. But if she's still running free, then you and I'll have the fun of competing for her."

"What 'competing' if you fire her?"

"There aren't any rules in this particular pursuit, Kade. I'll play my cards. You play yours."

Not bothering to respond, Kade punched *end*.

* * * * *

Play your cards. Rylan's parting shot again rang through Kade. When he'd reached home, he'd spent a couple of hours getting his new stock settled in and the orphan in the same pen with a motherly cow he kept around for just such situations, then he'd gone into his office to deal with the never-ending paperwork. The Pendleton rodeo in eastern Oregon was coming up in a couple of weeks. As one of the premiere rodeos in the country, it drew the top riders. They deserved and would get the best bulls and broncs.

Finally, thankfully, he'd accomplished everything he needed to for one day. He reached for the phone to call Maita, then stopped and again listened to the recorded message.

"You're a hard man to track down," the young female voice on the answering machine purred. "But if what I hear is right, it'll be worth it. You come highly recommended. My friend and I have a proposition to make. Two not quite for the price of one. Oh hell, you name the price—we're rich. Well, not as rich as we'd like to be. We're looking to increase what we can charge customers for our *services*. We want to offer them full and complete access to a couple of submissive beauties, beauties who know the boundaries and rules of the game." She finished by providing phone numbers.

Not long ago the thought of having two women at his disposal would have spurred his imagination with possibilities. Now he groaned.

He jotted down the women's numbers but instead of calling them, he dialed Maita's cabin. It rang four times before he heard her breathless "Hello."

"It's me," he said. "Did I interrupt something?"

"I was packing."

"Then you're really leaving?"

"How did you— Oh, that's right. You and my former boss are friends."

"Not friends," he corrected. He explained about the conversation he'd had with Rylan and ended by saying Rylan hadn't expected her to quit. "He knows how you feel about horses. He figured you'd accept his offer as long as you can keep doing what you love."

"Then I'm not really fired?"

"No."

"I see," she said after a brief silence. "I'm glad you're back," she whispered.

"Good." A plan started taking shape, a way of getting her to make a decision. If it turned out to be the right one— Damn it, it had to be! He had no experience in other ways of holding onto women. "I want to see you, as soon as possible."

"You do?" She sounded uncertain.

"Yeah." He hung up.

* * * * *

Maita was sitting on the small porch in front of her cabin when Kade drove up. She'd come out here because she hated looking at her half-packed suitcases. She'd much rather look out at the corrals, barns, and pasture that constituted Rylan's operation. She'd fallen in love with the wide-open spaces and the multitude of horses she'd been given responsibility for. Since going to work for Rylan, her desire, her need to pit herself against a bareback bronc had decreased probably because her work satisfied her, fulfilled her.

Then Kade got out of his truck and she knew work had little to do with her shift in focus. She'd seen a few stallions walk like that—sure, proud, confident. Most unneutered male horses lived ruled by their sexuality and often became unmanageable, but some proudly accepted what set them apart from the geldings. Even when brought to stud, they retained a measure of dignity. Their strength and restraint calmed the mares, resulting in a well-orchestrated breeding instead of a frenzy of hooves, teeth, muscle and cock.

"You don't want to leave," Kade said as he positioned himself in front of her.

She should have stood, done something to decrease his impact on her senses. "I haven't decided," she evaded.

"I don't appreciate being given the kind of ultimatum he did."

"You're not going to change Rylan's nature."

"No, I'm not," she agreed. She debated asking him to sit, but if she did, he might know how much power he had over her, power she didn't want inflicted, did she? "Ah, what did you want to see me about?" *Dumb, dumb, dumb.*

"I'm not sure I can answer that." He shifted position so his shins brushed her knees. "I haven't touched a woman since the last time I saw you."

Just like that—the rules have been laid down. "It didn't have to be. I'm sure you could have had your pick of—"

"There weren't any women where I was."

"Too bad. I'm sorry you're horny. And you think you can scratch your itch on me?"

"I want it to be more than that."

Stop saying those things! Don't you know I can't think around you? "What do you mean by more?"

He didn't respond but placed his hands on her chair arms and leaned toward her. He didn't stop until scant inches separated their mouths. She could have turned aside. She would have if she hadn't needed what he was offering.

"You understand what Rylan is proposing, don't you?" he asked. "The job you've always wanted in exchange for being his sex slave."

"I'm not interested."

"In him or in the sex?"

His words trailed over her, heating her. She thought she understood verbal foreplay, but Kade changed the rules. Hell, he created his own. "Neither," she belatedly replied.

"Are you sure? I've seen you turned on. You're a sexual creature."

"With a brain," she retorted. "If he thinks he can control me because he pays my salary, he's mistaken."

"Are you going to tell him that?"

How did Kade expect her to think with him standing over her and challenging her with his sexuality? "I shouldn't have to," she finally came up with. "If he can't figure it out on his own, I can't help him."

"It isn't that easy, Maita." Leaning closer, he began what she thought would be a kiss. But after touching his lips to hers, he closed his teeth over her lower lip and drew it into his mouth. Instantly, all argument, all discussion faded from her mind. She wanted one thing on this earth—him. To belong to him again.

"You can't switch off your sexuality that easily," he said after releasing her. He continued to loom over her. "You're ruled by what's between your legs."

"How can you say that!" she demanded. Even as she threw the words at him, she felt herself heat there. If he touched her cunt, no way could she hide her reaction. "Damn it, Kade, just because you've become an expert in whatever the hell it is you do doesn't mean all women are wired to respond in the same way." She gave fleeting thought to getting to her feet and ordering him to leave. Instead, she licked her lips and struggled not to look down at the juncture to his legs.

"No," he said, not moving an inch, "all women aren't built the same. But once the layer of civilization is stripped away, one thing remains—their sexuality."

She glared at him but couldn't think of a single word to throw at him.

"You want me to demonstrate?" he asked. He straightened and brought his features back into focus. Damn! Everything about him served as a challenge to her sanity. "A little test?"

"What...kind of test?"

* * * * *

Stupid, stupid, stupid, she kept silently repeating. Unfortunately, even as the words echoed inside her, she stood in her bedroom like some damn dumb animal being led to slaughter while Kade handcuffed her hands behind her. She didn't ask why he'd brought cuffs with him, neither did she ask what he had in mind.

Once the cuffs were in place, Kade turned her so she could see her reflection in the dresser mirror. He'd already removed her blouse but had left her bra in place. Her eyes had a trapped look—and more. At first she denied the other message, then gave in. *Give me the ride of my life*, she read in her reflection. *Take me places I've never been before.*

"Sit on the edge of your bed," Kade ordered.

"What are you—"

"Sit! Now!"

Shaking, she did as he ordered. As soon as she'd sunk into the mattress, he knelt before her and lifted first one leg and then the other so he could remove her boots and socks.

"Stand."

"Kade, what—"

"Stand!"

Mouth dry but another area of her anatomy in a decidedly different condition, she complied.

"Now," he said, his tone a mix of calm and command, "you are going to remove your jeans and panties."

"How can I? My hands—"

"No arguing! You *will* do as I order!" He grabbed her hair and yanked her head back. "Your braid's your undoing. As long as I hold it, I can make you do anything."

"Kade!"

"Listen to me! You still have a lot to learn about what's required of you."

"And if I don't want?"

"You won't know until you've experienced it. This is how you'll truly discover what's required of a submissive. You're teetering on the edge, wanting to step over but afraid."

"No!"

"Yes." He forced her to arch her neck even more. At the same time, he pulled her bra up over her breasts. "Are you going to obey, or am I going to have to force you?"

She already felt forced enough, thank you very much. Besides, truth was, she could hardly wait to see what he had planned. The cuffs allowed for some play between her hands, and although she had to contort her body this way and that to accomplish her goal, once he let go of her braid, she managed to unzip her jeans. She became something of a stripper as she slowly worked the fabric over her hips, then wriggled and turned until they were bunched around her ankles. Sitting again, she pushed them all the way off with her toes. By then she felt divorced from her anatomy — except for the heat between her legs.

The whole time, he'd stood a few feet away, watching.

"Now the panties."

No more cloth against my crotch. Open to him. Accessible.

Unable to think beyond those flashes of comprehension, she sent the pale blue panties along the same path her jeans had taken.

"Sit down — on the chair."

The only chair in the small room was better suited for a dining room because it was wooden with a straight back and legs with no cushion. She started to plant her ass on the hard seat, but Kade grabbed her arms and positioned them so they were behind the back rest.

"What are —" she started to ask but stopped when he glared at her. She'd tried not to think about the lengths of rope he'd brought into the room, but when he selected one and stepped behind her, nothing else mattered. Although she couldn't see what he was doing, she had no doubt of his intention. Using movements that put her in mind of an experienced calf roper, he ran a rope from her wrists down to the rear leg stretcher.

"I could gag you," he informed her when he'd finished. "And I might. Never lose sight of that. The moment you say something I don't want to hear, I'll silence you."

Silent. Helpless. But because Kade offered something far different from what had once been forced on the child she'd been, she nodded.

"Good. I suggest you speak only when I give you permission, but sometimes it might not be possible. Next, legs spread."

Spread. Her cunt accessible. She shook as she complied by hooking her feet around the chair legs. Her tremors kicked up a notch when he tied her in place. As long as she remained still, the ropes around her ankles didn't chafe, but she had to stay on her toes for comfort.

"A compliant little sex slave, aren't you?" He unceremoniously stroked her labia. "A hungry bitch willing to do whatever her master orders." His fingers slid over her slit. As if rewarding the invasion, she felt her cunt let down, bathing him.

"Doesn't take much to get you going, does it," he observed. For a length of time she couldn't define, he stroked, caressed, sometimes probed. Her entire pussy belonged to him.

No, she acknowledged from deep inside the sensual world he'd spun over her, more than her pussy had given itself up to him. She'd surrendered her freedom, her voice, certainly her dignity to this man when she'd never believed that possible. At the same time, he'd freed her from her past.

And her body screamed for more.

"I'll be back," he said abruptly.

Belatedly comprehending that he no longer had his hand on her, she straightened as best she could and stared. The little room was empty. He'd left her alone and helpless, spread-eagled and hot.

Kade! Don't leave me like this! I need —

She'd been about to admit she needed sex, but with her cunt now untouched and unstimulated, she saw herself as he must—as anyone who came in would. She'd allowed herself to be turned into an object. She'd become little more than a dripping sex organ.

Damn, damn, damn! What a compliant little slut he's turned you into.

Still, when he returned, she would have launched herself into his arms if she could have. He'd removed his shirt and jeans. His straining cock remained hidden if obvious beneath his briefs. His hands were behind him, holding something.

"I've been exploring," he said. "And I found something, actually several somethings." With a flourish, he held out her assortment of vibrators. "I haven't tested the batteries, but I'm guessing you know which ones are in operating order. Decision time, my little slave. Which is your favorite?"

Which one do you want me to use on you, she heard. Her vision blurred. She saw smears of silver, pink, black, everything from a compact bullet to a simulated penis. "I, ah, the blue pearlescent one," she managed.

"Ah, because of the nub on the end—an efficient probe made for contact with your clit."

Don't make me think — Oh god, touch me with it and I'll —

"Interesting because I initially would have made the same choice." Although she didn't need a demonstration, he placed the metallic nub against hers and turned it on. Sensation slammed into her. Trying to watch him and lose herself in pleasure at the same time splintered her.

"However—" He silenced the vibrator. "I found something I like even better."

"Kade, please!" She lifted her buttocks off the seat in a desperate effort to present herself to him.

"Patience!"

He again went into the bathroom, and she thought she'd explode while waiting for him. The longer he was gone, the more she believed he was doing this on purpose, drawing out the suspense until she'd do anything for him. Her so-called uncle had once played the same game by withdrawing what passed for affection from him to say nothing of food and sleep until she complied. The difference between then and now, she told herself, was that she hadn't wanted to do what she had so long ago.

But, damn it, admitting she was ruled by her need for stimulation and satisfaction unsettled her. She'd spent so many years and so much effort building her self-esteem and self-respect. And now she was throwing it away, handing herself over to a man she didn't understand.

She sensed his presence before her eyes focused. His pace was slow, and his gaze remained, not on her naked and accessible body, but her face. When he again stood close enough to easily touch her everywhere, he showed her his latest possession.

"I'm not surprised you have this," he said of the muscle massager she sometimes relied on after a particularly rough day. "It goes with the lifestyle, doesn't it?"

"Lifestyle?"

"Not bondage if that's what you're thinking." He laid the vibrator on the chair between her legs.

She struggled not to gape at it. "I—wasn't. I've never—"

"Never used it on your pussy?"

"No."

"Good. I want this to be your first time." Leaving her, he went to a low table where she'd set up her stereo system. He unplugged the extension cord from the stereo and brought it, still connected to the wall socket, back with him. He let her see him plug the massager into the cord. "Believe me, by the time I'm done, you'll wonder why you waited."

Picking up the massager, he turned it on. A quiet humming filled the air and assaulted her senses. She knew what he intended to do with it. Still, when he touched it to her mons, she tried to escape by pushing herself against the back of the chair and closing her legs as much as the ankle ropes would allow. She fought the impact on her sex by holding her breath.

"It won't work, Maita," Kade informed her. He increased the pressure. "There isn't a woman alive who can stop her body from reacting. It's instinct, physical, animal."

Animal. She'd seen more than her share of brood mares with their tails high in the air, vaginas dripping, flinging their heads at the sky and prancing on nervous hooves. Their excitement had filled the air with energy and sent an unmistakable message to any stallions in the area.

Sucking in desperately needed air, Maita surrendered to sensation. Head back and legs again splayed, she felt imprisoned by movement. Kade was right—the massager produced a punch her vibrators had only hinted it. When using them, she'd had to work and encourage her vagina before she could hope to orgasm. Even with fresh batteries, she'd had to resort to fantasy by imagining herself in the arms of some hunk with an oversized cock. But the massager...god, she could be half-dead and she'd still respond!

The moment he slid it from her mons to the entrance to her sex, her cunt muscles started clenching. She knew nothing beyond reaction, beyond this breakneck race to a climax.

"Stop, stop, stop," she chanted. "I can't take, can't take—"

"Yes, you can. You're going to."

All right, she silently agreed. *I surrender. Bring it on.*

He did or maybe all credit lay with the muscle relaxer. Now she fought her bonds, not because she wanted freedom, but because she couldn't remain still. Arching her spine but keeping her legs apart, she rose a few inches off the chair. When her spine couldn't handle the strain anymore, she collapsed.

But the massager kept after her, pushing her to the edge and beyond.

The climax rolled out of and over her, waves going on and on. She heard herself scream. The cry, like her climax, seemed endless.

"Breathe," Kade ordered. "Breathe."

She did. At least she thought she did. Her head cleared enough to realize he hadn't freed her from assault. Even more overwhelming, he kicked up the massager's power. Her climax reached a new level. She was drowning, a small creature caught in a hurricane.

"No, no, no."

"Yes."

Because he controlled everything, she rode this new wave. Electricity burned throughout her. Her pussy became an out-of-control monster, pleasure and pain swirling together as one.

"Please, please, please."

"You want me to stop?"

"Yes!"

"What will you do for me then?"

"Anything! Anything." She whimpered the last.

"All right. Don't fight. Just experience."

Feeling as if she'd been struck with a cattle prod, she somehow latched onto his words. Because she had no control over her muscles anyway, she hadn't tried to fight the assault. Now she stopped thinking, stopped trying to anticipate, to keep from dying. Instead, she rocked to the ecstasy-waves and became them. She started grunting. Her cunt muscles continued to contract and release in waves, but they were becoming weaker. She felt wrapped in hues of gray and black.

"I won't let anything happen to you," she heard Kade say. "I'd never hurt you."

She felt lightheaded. "I'm going to…"

Chapter Eleven

Kade untied Maita and half-carried, half-led her to her bed. He placed her in a sitting position so he could unfasten her bra then helped her lay down. *Are you all right?* he wanted to ask but self-doubt kept him silent. No, not self-doubt he amended as he brushed strands of hair back from her cheeks. Right now he pretty much hated himself.

Why? This was hardly the first time he'd forced an explosive and long-lasting climax from a woman. The others had admitted how much they loved the experience, and he couldn't remember how many had asked for a repeat performance. Sometimes he accommodated them. Sometimes he didn't.

But never before had he felt as if he'd been experiencing the same thing.

"Do you want to go to sleep?" he asked as he sat beside her. "I'll leave you alone if you do."

"No!" She grabbed his arm with unexpected strength. "Stay here."

"I'd think you'd be glad to be rid of me."

She shook her head and repositioned herself so she was on her side and looking up at him. "I'm afraid to be by myself, with myself."

Not sure he understood what she was getting at, he unabashedly studied her. She looked so damn small around livestock. Even with her strong shoulders and

Vonna Harper

muscled arms, her body was made for comforting. He might not think that if he didn't know what she'd endured as a child, but he did.

"Should I have given you more warning?" he asked. "Allowed you more say in what happened?"

"Why did you do it?" she asked and sat up.

"You wanted it, didn't you?" he sidestepped.

"Answer me, Kade!"

He couldn't, could he? But she kept studying him, her nude body so damn close. "Several reasons," he said although he didn't know when, or if, he'd ever tell her all of them. "Mostly to bring you pleasure."

"Pleasure? What about torture? Kade, I haven't paid you for orgasms. Our relationship is different, at least I hope it is."

"Is it?" he whispered.

"We haven't defined it. Maybe because neither of us understands what's happening. Oh, don't get me wrong. I'll never forget what I just experienced." She swiped between her legs, the contact gentle against her sensitive organs. "But I'd never think of-of playing with the sanity of someone I cared about."

You care about me? Maybe...love?

"It's what I know how to do," he admitted, hating himself.

"I'm sorry," she muttered and drew him close.

"Sorry?"

"Never mind." She sighed and kissed him but kept the contact brief. "I need a shower. Please, will you be here when I return?"

"If you want me."

* * * * *

What had that conversation been about? Maita debated as she left the bathroom. She hadn't rushed her shower because she'd needed time to think and had told Kade she didn't want him coming in with her because she needed her own space.

Well, she'd gotten both those things, only they hadn't done her a damn bit of good.

Even clean with her just-shampooed hair still damp and no clothes rubbing her sensitive flesh, she felt no closer to understanding herself than she had when she'd gotten off her bed.

Then she saw him. Although he'd gotten dressed, he was stretched out on his back on her bed, hands behind his head and staring at the ceiling. She knew this was what she needed to be doing. Nothing else existed — for now.

"Solving the world's problems, are you?" she asked. She was the one looking down at him. Maybe she should feel as if their roles had been reversed, but she didn't.

"Your clothes — "

"Later. First, I need to deal with yours." She crawled onto the bed, pushing against his hips to get him to make room for her. While he studied her, she unfastened his jeans and began the disrobing that had become such a core part of their relationship. He assisted by lifting his hips. Once she'd discarded his garments, she stretched out beside him and rested an arm on his thighs.

He hadn't lost anything of his erection. Caressed by lamplight, she saw the beauty in his penis. Although his hair was a deep, rich brown, his pubic hair had been touched with lighter colors. He wasn't particularly hairy. His lean hips and muscle-only thighs combined to make his cock look more dominant—either that or she'd be drawn to the organ no matter what its appearance.

She slid a hand under his scrotum and supported the weight of his balls. "I love the feel. The substance."

He muttered something unintelligible.

"I can't duplicate what you did to—for me," she admitted. "I wouldn't know how to begin."

"I'm not asking you to."

But, she believed, he'd stayed here because he wanted to fuck, to have sex, maybe to make love. She longed to ask if he ever thought of her in terms of love but was afraid of the answer. Maybe, maybe she could get their bodies to speak to each other.

"Sit up, please," she asked.

He didn't move so she scooted away and sat herself. Looking puzzled, he finally did as she asked.

"I want to see the look on your face when we have sex," she told him. "And for you to know what I'm experiencing."

"You're ready for—"

"You are. That's what matters."

Maybe she saw what she needed to, but she chose to believe the wanting in his eyes. "You did this before." His voice held a note of wonder. "The last time I'd worked you, when I was done, you turned things around and put the focus on me."

"Why wouldn't I?"

He studied her. "Why would you?"

Because I'm falling in love with you, she admitted before another thought touched her. Was it possible none of his *clients* had given him consideration?

"Once," she admitted, "when I was a child, I didn't think beyond myself—surviving. But I've changed since I got free. I've learned horses are capable of giving and receiving love and I'm starting...I'm starting to believe humans are the same."

"And you consider me a human?"

"Yes. Oh yes," she said and kissed him. After a moment, he returned the gesture, tentative at first, but soon he wrapped his arms around her and held her close. Because the mattress wasn't particularly firm, they sagged against each other.

Having recently been royally machine-fucked had left her body humming along in first gear. She sensed her potential to shift into overdrive but was in no hurry. Instead, she dismissed her own needs and focused on Kade. His question about his worthiness bothered her.

Although she was content to remain in his arms, she forced herself to pull back. He kept a hand on her hip, her nails trailed over his ribs. "You are a beautiful man," she told him. "Certainly handsome but also beautiful."

"You need glasses."

Guessing her comment had made him uncomfortable, she clarified by stroking his throat, shoulders, chest and belly. Her every touch caused him to suck in a breath, his cock shuddered. "Your body is perfect. Perfect," she repeated when he started to speak. "And yes, I'm including your scars because they're part of you." Knowing she'd said this or something like it before, she ran her fingers into his pubic hair. "Have you ever seen a wolf?" she asked.

"In the wild, you mean?" He rested his own hand on her mons and cradled it in his palm.

Oh my god! "Wild or a preserve. Not a zoo."

"I thought I did once when I was in Canada, but I'm not sure."

Where had she been going with this? Oh yes. "You — Sometimes you make me think of a wolf. When you're hunting..." He'd given her mons a gentle rub. Waiting for a repeat performance briefly stopped her. Then she returned the *favor* by sliding her fingers around the base of his cock but not touching the organ itself. "When you're hunting, or working a woman, you're a confident predator. Dangerous and single-minded."

"Like this?" Although she sat on her folded legs, he managed to slide his forefinger over her labia.

"Y-es."

He stroked her again then turned his attention back to her mons. "Just checking. All right. Your point is?"

Damn him! He was playing with her, demonstrating his understanding and mastery of a woman's body. Not allowing her to forget what he'd brought to this bed.

Cupping his scrotum and closing her hand firmly around it pulled his attention off her sex organs. Although she didn't particularly like things this way, she continued. "I used to volunteer at a preserve in central Oregon. Part of my chores included checking the wolves every morning, making sure they were all right." She relaxed her fingers slightly but maintained her hold on his balls. "When they're feeding or getting ready to feed, I wouldn't want to be anywhere near them. It-it's not quite like that when you've immobilized me because you don't have their fangs and claws."

He laughed, removed his hand from her mons and leaned back, propping himself up with his arms and giving her full access to him.

She repositioned herself so she sat in the opposite direction from him. Leaning over him, she shifted her ministrations to his shaft. The weight, warmth, and pulsing veins fascinated her. "But wolves spend only a little while as predators. The rest of the time they're part of a pack, interacting, showing affection, love."

Under her fingers, his cock turned into steel. When she ran a finger over its tip, she found a droplet waiting for her. She could house him, fulfill him, give him release—both of them.

"They can be gentle," she said.

"I'm not."

"Aren't you? I've watched you with calves and foals. And your relationship with your ranch hands—they're loyal because you treat them like equals."

"It's not the same thing."

Why was he arguing with her? Instead of asking, she shifted so she was now on her elbows and knees, her mouth near his cock. Forcing him to take his hand off her mons hadn't been the brightest idea she'd ever had. But, she reminded herself, she'd already had her turn. Had she ever!

While he watched, she leaned down and licked his tip. She wanted to hold his cock so she could direct its movement, but if she did, she risked losing her balance. Licking, retreating, briefly closing her lips around what she could of his cock more than entertained her. From the way he kept lifting himself toward her, he felt the same way.

"No more," she admitted at last. She didn't tell him her ass felt damn lonely sticking up in the air without his hands on it. Instead, she again changed position. This time she settled her bottom between his outstretched legs, her own legs over and around his hips and her feet touching his hands. She leaned back.

"There," she said unnecessarily. "Now we're closer."

He indicated the scant distance between his cock and her cunt. "Not close enough."

"I have a suggestion—if you're ready."

He indicated his cock. "*If?*"

Even as she lifted her hips, she faced facts—in their times together, she'd seldom directed the flow and content of what they did. Even now, she half expected him to throw her against the bed and force himself into her. When he allowed her to remain in control, she helped direct the angle of entry by bracing her hands on his ankles. He strained toward her but didn't scoot closer, his body language saying the next move was hers. Throwing aside all caution and remnants of modesty, she pushed forward.

His cock tip pressed against her labia then found entrance. She inched closer, her buttocks riding over his thighs. His invasion of her increased. She dimly realized he'd captured her ankles, the grip holding her against him. She'd never fucked like this before and hadn't known what to expect. Hell, she'd barely known what she was doing.

Now, looking at him with their sex organs joined, she wondered if she'd deliberately chosen a position that required them to watch each other.

Required? No, allowed.

Her weight on his thighs restricted his movements, but after a couple of false starts, they began rocking back and forth. Once she'd locked onto the movement, she started contracting and relaxing her cunt muscles. Easy at first but then with more focus, she visualized squeezing his cock. She tried to develop a rippling muscle action, but his size inside her, his eyes probing her every mood, splintered her concentration.

Rocking, rocking, rocking, holding his ankles so she wouldn't fall back and find her pussy empty. Feeling his fingers locked around her ankles, watching his body's movements as he probed her vagina. She'd never looked at him like this before, never lost touch with all restraint and allowed her eyes to say it all.

You fill me. Fulfill me. I trust you with everything.

The familiar wet heat of a pending climax hummed through her.

I'm coming, his expression revealed. *Coming. Leaving something of me in you.*

Something of me inside you?

"We-we didn't use a condom," she breathed.

"Too late." He exploded inside her, a heated sperm bath filling her. As he continued to climax, she dove into her own sensations. Her cunt muscles worked him. She wanted only one thing—to record for all the time the feel of him inside her, to take possession of his semen and float to her own climax on it.

No longer able to focus, she closed her eyes and lived in sensation. He started to deflate, but she kept him in her, cradling him in soft, wet tissue. She'd become accustomed to explosive climaxes around him, but this one had a lazy quality, a reminder of long summer evenings with a breeze whispering over her flesh and the song of night creatures in the air. She could stay like this forever, as one with the man who'd changed her.

But finally her ride ended.

Because there was no hurry, she opened her eyes and found him gazing at her. Neither moved. "Damn it," he said although his voice sounded emotionless. "I know better than to get carried away. If you get pregnant..."

Pregnant. A child. A life to nurture and nourish. Someone to belong to.

"I told you, I'm on the pill."

"Douche."

He didn't want a child. Of course he didn't.

"All right," she whispered and left him.

* * * * *

Crying, Maita washed Kade's seed out of her. By the time she'd finished and taken a shower, she'd retained enough control over her emotions to function. Thinking to apply makeup to hide the residues of her tears, she wiped steam off the mirror. Only when she dropped the towel to the floor did she realize she hadn't brought in any clothes. It didn't matter. He'd seen her naked more times than she could recall.

What was she doing? What had just happened? Kade dominated her, wanted her for everything except the real world where pregnancy changed sex partners into parents and taught them the full meaning of ever after.

Why should he be any different from her parents?

Face facts, Maita. You came into this relationship alone. You'll leave it the same way.

After applying moisturizer, she reached for her limited collection of cosmetics with a shaking hand but stopped when she heard male voices. Walking over to the door, she listened.

Rylan.

Because she had no choice, she simply wrapped the towel around her before stepping into the room. Kade lay naked and unselfconscious on her bed. Rylan stood in the doorway. As she joined them, Rylan shifted his attention from Kade to her. A bemused expression spread over his face.

"Looks like I interrupted something." He pointed at the towel. "A little late, am I? Round one is over."

"What do you want?" she demanded. She glanced at Kade but couldn't read his expression. Maybe she didn't want to.

"I could say I'm here for a piece of the action, but that would be crude, wouldn't it? Honest but crude." Rylan reached for but didn't touch the terrycloth covering her breasts. "What the hell's the deal, Maita? You won't spread your legs for me, but Kade's in your bed. You're playing favorites."

"Shut the fuck up," Kade bit out.

"Who I sleep with and when is none of your damn business," she told her former boss.

"Under normal circumstances, I'd agree, but it's different when it comes to Kade and me, isn't it, old buddy."

"Get the hell out of here." Kade swung off the bed and stalked toward Rylan.

Rylan refused to give way. "Not yet, good buddy, not yet."

"What did you do?" she demanded. "Walk in without knocking?"

"Sure." Rylan shrugged. "It wouldn't be the first time."

An icy feeling washed through her. Sick, she turned on Kade. "What is he saying?"

"Nothing. Damn it, Rylan, get the fuck out of here."

"No!" she insisted. "I have every right to know what you're talking about. The two of you have, what, used the same woman at the same time?" She felt sick.

"Technically speaking, no," Rylan supplied while Kade glared. "I believe that's anatomically impossible although since women have more than one opening…" he indicated her mouth and then her ass, "…it's been known to happen."

"Don't play games," she managed through clenched teeth. She'd begun to shake. "What have the two of you done together?"

"Nothing," Kade snapped. "He's watched me at work, that's all."

"All?" Rylan snorted. "It was more intense than that, a hell of a lot more. For your information, missy, your fuck partner here likes an audience. And why shouldn't he?"

Kade had perfected the art of whatever the hell it was he did for a living. An act she'd always considered private was something he believed suitable for public display. From the night she'd met him, he'd kept her off balance. She barely knew which way was up around him. Whatever had made her think that she, an innocent to the dark world Kade and Rylan lived in, had any place in it?

She didn't belong there! She'd certainly never surrender her freedom to some man determined to force a climax from her. A man who wanted nothing to do with tomorrow.

Feeling as if she was clinging to the edge of a cliff, she turned her back on both men, walked over to where she'd put her suitcases and yanked on the first garments she found. Numb, she faced the men. Rylan had an amused, half-aroused expression. She couldn't read anything of Kade's thoughts.

Of course.

"I'm leaving," she said. "Rylan, I'll let you know where to send my last paycheck. Kade… Kade, I gave you everything and got nothing in return."

"Except for his cum," Rylan said.

"Shut up," she and Kade said at the same time. "Nothing of your heart," she added.

Chapter Twelve

As she'd done since she'd left Klamath three weeks ago, Maita spent the time before her ride at the Pendleton rodeo not behind the chutes but among the trailers, campers, and trucks belonging to contestants and their families. She should be accustomed to the sight of wives, girlfriends, children, dogs, even parents, but the past three weeks had been hard.

Her attention settled on a tiny girl in a stroller. Dressed in a frilly pink dress with a slightly askew pink bonnet covering what appeared to be a nearly bald head, the little one looked overwhelmed by the mass of legs churning around her. Suddenly the girl broke into a grin and began clapping. Large, leathered hands reached down and drew her out of the stroller.

Maita couldn't hear what the cowboy was saying, but there was no mistaking the man's unabashed love. He nibbled a tiny nose, the girl squealed and wrapped her arms around his neck.

Daddy.

Blinking back tears, Maita pivoted and walked away. She'd gotten a note from Kade the other day, a few lines telling her he'd gotten the number for the Pendleton post office box she'd rented from Rylan. He'd given her his cell phone number and asked her to get in touch if she hadn't gotten her period.

She had.

Was Kade here? she pondered. After a moment of denial she faced facts. He was supplying this year's stock—of course he'd accompany them. And it certainly hadn't taken more than adding one and one for him to determine she intended to compete in the rodeo.

She shouldn't have sent in this particular entry fee, damn it. She knew better! In the past three weeks she'd participated in four smaller rodeos. The first time out she'd been thrown but had finished in the money after that. When she was riding—or trying to—she thought of nothing except competing. During the mental and physical preparations she felt alive again, reconnected with her passion. Only afterward did she acknowledge her pain. But the three-day Pendleton rodeo included one of the largest purses, and she needed the money.

"You're Maita Compton, aren't you?" a woman asked.

Maita looked at the fresh-faced newcomer. Maybe she should ask how she managed to keep her white outfit spotless. "Yes," she said.

"I knew it." The newcomer stuck out her hand. "I'm Sandy Mercer. I've been participating in barrel racing since I was a child but hearing about you gave me the courage to try the riding events. You're my hero."

My hero. Maita feel old. "I appreciate the compliment," she said. "Is this your first time on a bronc?"

Sandy explained that she'd been riding all her life and competed in a number of unsanctioned rodeos but had never gone after money before. "I'm scared to death," she admitted. "But I figure it's time we women gave the cowboys a run for their money, right? I hope you don't mind me competing against you."

"Not at all. You're doing bareback?" Sandy was tall and slim with narrow shoulders and slender arms.

"No. I'm not that cra— I mean, I'm not that brave. I need a saddle under me."

They chatted for a few more minutes, or mostly Sandy explained how her parents had encouraged her various interests while she was growing up. They'd always made sure she had the best barrel horses they could afford, and her mother had made her outfit. "They're less than crazy about what I'm doing now," she admitted, "but I need a challenge. To prove myself."

Maita couldn't say whether Sandy would make it, but she wished her all the best. From what Sandy had said, she suspected the younger woman was prompted more by rebellion against the sheltered world her parents had provided than a true competitive spirit. Still, talking to Sandy had allowed her to briefly break free of her inner turmoil. Sandy's story had also brought her face-to-face with the difference between having parents and what she'd experienced.

Restlessness, or maybe something else, took her behind the chutes. A handful of women but mostly cowboys milled about. The stock handlers went about their work with a mix of determination and profanity while the competitors stood out because of their nervous intensity. Her own nerves resided where she couldn't reach them. Either that or the question of when—not if— she'd run into Kade had distracted her from less important concerns. *Ride. Prove your competitive spirit to him. Show him you don't need what he offered.*

The thoughts became her mantra. If a cowboy looked as if he needed someone to talk to, she engaged him in a bantering conversation. If he stood off to himself in silent contemplation or prayer, she simply acknowledged him with a nod. A stock handler pulled her aside and gave her a piece of advice about the bronc she'd drawn, and she committed what he told her about BossLady's habit of tucking her head between her legs to memory. According to the handler, BossLady was a new acquisition with little experience in the arena but bullheaded and incorrigible.

"She ain't got no use for humans," the tobacco-chewing handler concluded. "Just flat-out hates people."

"Is that true?" Maita asked the broad-backed mare as she perched on the top of the chute BossLady had just been placed in. "You'd rather send me into the next county as eat?"

BossLady responded by flinging her head skyward. Maita leaned away but kept her attention on the mare. For a moment human and animal locked eyes. *This is what I live for*, Maita told the mare. *Pitting myself against you makes me feel alive.*

I hate you, BossLady replied.

Appreciative of the honesty, Maita straddled the broad back. She clamped her knees against the mare's sides, her buttocks not quite touching BossLady's backbone. As had happened countless times before, all existence beyond this moment evaporated.

At her signal, the chute gate opened. BossLady stood unmoving. Then something ignited inside her, and she all but levitated in her determination to find freedom. Head so low her muzzle nearly dragged the ground, BossLady kicked with her hind legs. From the first buck, Maita found the mare's rhythm. Although the horse also spun in circles, the flip, flip, flip of her hindquarters never let up. Sitting as straight as possible, Maita pumped her knees up and down, up and down, the dull rowels on her spurs rolling easily over the tough hide. With her free hand, she reached toward where she believed the sky to be. Her right arm and shoulder took the greatest punishment.

She lost track of time and saw nothing except a blur. At one point, her head jerked down, and she cracked her chin on her collarbone. Some demented part of her brain insisted on counting the number of bucks, but as soon as she got to three, she lost track and had to begin again. Her arm and shoulder screamed. Her knees burned.

And she stayed on.

Finally, mercifully, she heard the buzzer signaling eight endless seconds had passed, and she grabbed the rigging with both hands. The moment BossLady had all four feet on the ground, Maita catapulted off. She landed solid, then fell to her knees. She scrambled onto her feet and whirled around. BossLady was already a dozen yards away running full-out for the exit gate.

"Would you look at that, ladies and gentlemen!" the announcer boomed. "Watch her, the rest of you cowboys. Maita knows how it's done."

It sounded as if everyone in the stands was applauding. Grinning and happy beyond belief, Maita reached for her hat so she could acknowledge the approval, but she'd lost it during the ride. After waving and smiling some more, she hurried over to the side to make room for the next rider.

According to the announcer, she was now in the lead for the first go-round, but she knew better than to start counting her winnings.

How do you like them apples, Kade? Just goes to show your brand of courtship didn't get in the way of what I'm determined to accomplish.

Courtship? Hardly.

Although none of the riders who came after her in the bareback event stayed on for the required time, some of her euphoria had dissipated by the time she'd been declared the night's winner. Her share of the purse would pay for three or four entry fees for upcoming rodeos, hardly enough to secure her future. And Kade's business didn't supply stock for the next two rodeos she intended to enter.

* * * * *

"Here's your hat."

Maita didn't move. Her hands remained in her back pockets, her gaze on the calves boy and girl contestants had demonstrated their roping and tying skills on earlier. The calves had recovered from their exertions and several were playfully butting heads. Night would soon blanket the rodeo grounds.

"Thank you," she said.

"I saw you ride," Kade told her.

"I wondered if you would."

"You did beautifully."

Touched by his soft tone, she faced him. His appearance made her think of the enduring, unchanging aspect of what it meant to be a cowboy. If she didn't know who and what he was, she might have told him he looked as if he'd been standing like this for hundreds of years. "I don't know if it was beautiful," she said. "But I'm pleased."

"You should be." He placed her hat on her head then gave her back her space. "You've been all right?"

"Fine."

He continued to study her, his gaze never moving below her neck. "Are you pregnant?" he asked.

"No."

He nodded. "It wouldn't have fit into your plans, would it?"

"Or in yours."

"I would have made it work," he muttered. "I've been thinking about what it would be like to be a father."

"You have?"

"I've never gone there before but—" When he touched the side of her neck, she thought of butterfly wings. His tone nearly did her in, as did his soft, dark eyes. "I asked Rylan," he continued after a telling moment. "He said he'd sent you your last paycheck. And you've won your share of small purses."

He'd been keeping tabs on her. Despite everything she'd told herself, her mind filled with images of what had happened the other times they'd been together. She couldn't remember why she'd left. Instead, she felt herself being drawn closer to him, melting into him. "I can't complain," she finally thought to say.

"Is this what you're going to do for a while?" he asked. Like her, he tucked his hands in his rear pockets. "Compete full-time?"

"I think so. If I don't get hurt, I figure I can make it."

"It'll be enough?"

He wasn't just talking about money. She had no doubt of it. "I'll make it enough."

"Is it what you want?"

What I want is you for my lover. To lose myself with you each night. But it's an insane fantasy.

Grateful he couldn't read her thoughts, she turned back to the corral full of calves. He joined her. "I love watching calves," he said. "They seem more intelligent when they're young, more interested in the world, energetic. Then they grow up and become complacent. Something is sucked out of them."

"Their bodies get heavier. It's harder to get around."

"I think it's more than that." He shrugged. "Maybe they realize this is all life is going to be."

"Complacent?"

"Resigned."

"Is this what you want to talk to me about?" she asked. "Your philosophy regarding cattle?"

"Of course not." He draped his arm over her shoulder.

Just like that her body remembered everything between them. Heat the evening breeze couldn't quiet built in her cheeks, and she felt her cunt soften.

"What happened?" he asked. "Something went wrong between us."

"I-I don't know if I understand everything."

"At least tell me what you do know."

If he'd ever probed deep into her like this before, she didn't recall. Telling herself it didn't matter because whatever they'd had was in the past tense, she dug deep. "I told you about my childhood, things I never thought I'd admit to another human being. I don't know…maybe it was because you robbed me of all privacy."

"I do that well, don't I?"

"Yes."

"If I hadn't pushed the buttons I did, I wouldn't know what that so-called uncle did to you. You would have kept your past buried."

"What are you getting at?"

"I'm not sure." He drew out the words then turned her toward him. Behind him, the moon was beginning to rise. It promised to be full. "I never expected— Hell, I'd have done anything to change what you went through! Monsters like him should be killed."

His emotion forced her beyond herself. He now held her in place via his arms around her waist. Her breasts brushed his ribs, and she felt his cock. With each heartbeat, she lost more of her separate self. If he was deliberately drawing her back into his world—

"Maita, for much of my life, I dealt with selfish, self-absorbed women. Maybe I came to believe all women are like that."

She struggled to make sense of what he was saying. At the same time her body whispered its own urgent message. "You never experienced anything else?" she managed. "What about your mother?"

Instead of answering, he released her and stepped back. She felt the loss throughout her. But much as she needed to feel flesh against flesh, she needed inside his mind and soul more. Without honesty from him—

"I have to go back to work," he said and extended a hand, palm up. "But when I'm done I'd like to tell you something—if you'll listen."

She laid her hand over his, but although she ached to lace her fingers with his, she left things as they were. "I will."

* * * * *

Maita had used some of her final paycheck from Rylan to buy a small travel trailer she now hauled behind her truck. She'd told Kade where she was parked, but although she could have used her time to clean up and try to make enough room inside the small space for him, she paced outside. The rodeo was over for the night, and the fans had left the stands. Various workmen milled about cleaning up, doing a few repairs, and preparing the grounds for tomorrow's events. She both appreciated the relative quiet and needed back the press of bodies. She wanted to talk to her fellow competitors, watch the family men with their families, smell the mix of livestock, hot dogs and popcorn. Mostly she needed too much movement for thought.

When, finally, the last loose board had been nailed back in place and the last worn-out light replaced, she wandered back to her trailer but still couldn't force herself into the confining space.

Kade had access to any woman he wanted. They not only beat a path to his door but paid him for exploring primitive aspects of their sensuality. In contrast, she hadn't given him what he'd come to expect. Oh, yes, she'd let him play with her and had cried out her response, but then she'd walked away from him.

I'll walk again, she told him. *If restraints and forced climaxes are all you have to offer, it isn't enough.*

Not enough?

Shaking, she looked around. She needed to run, but even if she could see where she was going, her riding boots weren't built for speed. Trapped in the outfit that had served her so well earlier, she absorbed tension and emotion. Being fucked wasn't enough. She needed more, something she'd never had and didn't believe Kade had ever given.

Maybe she heard him approaching. Maybe her nerves recorded his presence. Whichever it was, she made fists of her fingers and faced him. He walked with the plodding pace of a man who has been on his feet since before dawn. His hat had slid forward, shielding his gaze. Her trailer had no outside lighting, and the nearest overhead light was too far away to rob him of his shadows.

"You're still up," he said. "I wasn't sure."

"Are you done for the night?"

"Done." He stopped with maybe three feet separating them. "Do you want to go inside or walk?"

"Walk."

He took her hand, and they headed toward the rear of the grounds where the livestock was kept. The last hint of humanity had been stripped from this part of the rodeo. A few cowboys might still be up and reliving their performances over a beer, but she knew most had gone to bed so they'd be ready for tomorrow. That Kade hadn't taken her need for sleep into consideration said something about what was going on in his mind. Unfortunately, she couldn't guess what it was.

"I kept thinking about the way things ended the last time we were together," he said at length. "Things said and not said."

"Things done?"

"Yes. That too."

They walked some more, ending up at the Brahma pen. Kade released her hand and gripped the railing. For several minutes they watched the shadows of the great animals. Most had bedded down. A couple were still eating while another groomed the back of one of the eaters, his teeth brushing lightly over leathery flesh.

"You remind me of one of them," she said because the silence was getting to her. "You don't have to do anything to convince people of your power."

"Money speaks?"

"Not just the size of your spread and checkbook although you have a point. Like them, you have a confidence about the way you handle yourself. When...when you were showing me what my body is capable of, not once did I sense any doubt."

"I know what I'm doing in that department."

Exhaustion dragged at her ability to concentrate, and she suspected he felt the same way. Not only had they put in a long, physical day but being around each other carried its own brand of stress, at least it did for her. If he wanted to fuck, she wasn't sure she could accommodate him—if he gave her the option.

No more. I've had enough of being manhandled.

A memory of standing helpless before him while he brought her to the edge of a sexual cliff and then catapulted her into space threatened to make her change her mind. But restraints and foreign objects were no substitute for the man himself. If he couldn't comprehend that—

"If you feel like listening, I want to tell you something," he said. "Something I've never told another human being. When I'm done, maybe you'll understand why I turned out the way I did."

Chapter Thirteen

Kade had been raised by a single parent. He'd never known his father and suspected his mother hadn't been sure of the man's identity. Given her line of work, Kade had never bothered to press for a list of possibilities.

"She loved hooking," he said. He was looking at her but night kept her from reading his mood. Still, his quiet, unemotional tone told her a great deal. "You hear about women who take up prostitution because some man forces them into it, they need to support a drug habit, or they lack job skills. But there are others who flat-out would rather fuck than do anything else. My mother was one of them and so were her friends, her colleagues as they called each other."

"You lived with her the whole time you were growing up?"

"Yes. Hard for you to comprehend, is it? I suppose if the authorities had known about me, they would have removed me but maybe not. My mother— Let's say she had connections."

Why are you telling me? What makes me dif—

"We moved a lot the first few years," he continued. "Most of the places are a blur in my mind, and I prefer not to go back there mentally anyway. Of course when I was little I didn't know that what my mother did to put food on the table was frowned upon in polite society and against the law. I just thought it was neat that I got to wear 'in' clothes."

"No one at school knew?"

"If they did, I wasn't aware. I remember... Once some boys asked who my mother's sugar daddy was. I think most people assumed she'd inherited money. I got good grades and didn't get in trouble so didn't make waves."

"But as you got older, you put things together?"

"Oh yeah. The light finally went on but it happened over time, bits and pieces of understanding so there was never a single traumatic moment. I accepted reality."

His hand lay on the railing so she covered his with hers. As before she kept the contact light, impersonal. Underneath, her emotions churned. She was dimly aware of her body's need to connect with his, but so far her reaction in that department remained under control.

"Did she love you?" she asked.

"In her own way, and as much as she was capable of." His muscles under her fingers tightened. "By her own admission, she was a bitch in heat. She couldn't help the way she was wired."

Raised by someone without the capacity for true love, just like her. "She's dead?"

"Cancer. She fought it for three years, but the beast won."

"How old were you?"

"Nineteen, a man."

She would have debated the issue if she hadn't been concerned she'd distract him. "What did you do after she died?"

"Went to college. Maita, my mother made an obscene amount of money doing what she did. And she was a hell of a good money manager. We lived well, and she'd bought several acres near Sacramento about the time I started junior high. She had a house built, and I continued to live there while I went to college. Then developers started knocking on the door asking me to sell the land. I finally did."

"And you used the proceeds to start the contracting business?"

Kade explained that he'd used his degree in animal husbandry to secure a job with a vet whose job it was to monitor the health of rodeo stock. The more he learned about the sport and what it took to make it succeed, the more convinced he became this was for him. After all, he had no one to account to. The proceeds from selling the property had been making money in investments, and he used that to buy out a contractor who wanted to retire. "I've never regretted the decision," he said. "But this isn't the whole story."

She'd known it wasn't.

"As you've learned," he continued, "I have two sides. This is the part no one else knows about."

"But people—women anyway—know what you do beyond feed livestock."

"True. But they don't understand why. I don't think any of them cared."

Leaning against his side, she draped his arm around her shoulder and wrapped her arm around his waist. They continued to stare at the livestock. "I do."

He took a deep breath. "From the moment you told me about your childhood, I realized you'd found something you trusted about me. I control a lot of women's bodies, but they don't hand me their minds, and I don't ask for them. With you, it was different."

"Maybe it's because we love the same thing." She indicated the Brahmas. "The world those creatures represent."

He didn't immediately respond. She hadn't considered the explanation before, but now it made sense. Only someone willing to supply bucking stock understood why she felt compelled to try to ride that stock. But their common ground went even deeper, back to their childhoods.

"You didn't say anything about your upbringing after I'd dumped on you," she said softly. "It bothered me."

"I knew it did."

She'd opened her mouth to ask what had kept him silent when he continued. "Maita, I learned a great deal about female sexuality from my mother because she didn't try to keep her career from me, but it wasn't just her. I mentioned that her friends were also hookers."

"Yes."

"My mother got sick about the time I became aware of the layers of complexity behind what she did. Just when my hormones kicked into high gear, the focus shifted from sex for a living to trying to keep her alive. Eventually she couldn't work, but her friends stepped in to help keep us going. When one of them needed a reliable male around for protection, I filled the bill."

"Oh." *Brilliant statement, just brilliant.*

"I went from playing bodyguard to sometimes watching, especially when things got kinky."

"The-the men didn't mind?"

"They weren't given a choice. Damn! I don't know what's so damn hard about telling you this."

"Your mother was dying."

Maybe it was her fingers pulling his shirt out of his waistband so she could stroke his flesh that kept him going. Maybe briefly standing on tiptoe and brushing her lips over his jawline helped the most. As the night marched on, and she felt more and more as if she was melting into him, he spoke of women who did the only thing they could to distract a young man first from his mother's slow dying and then the aftermath of her death. They brought him into their world. And when he showed interest in the edgier, more dangerous aspects of hooking, they encouraged him. Under their tutelage, he learned the finer art of bridging the gap between capture fantasies and the real thing. Because they insisted on it, he learned how to judge a woman's limits and never took anyone too far. He went from observer to student to practitioner to master of the dark arts.

"They trusted me because they'd known me since I was a child. I respected them," he said. "I learned that the bar measuring so-called civilized behavior can be moved by degrees—for everyone's pleasure."

"And your profit," she ventured.

He shrugged and squeezed her shoulder. "Eventually. That kind of evolved. Now you know why I'm where I am today."

"You've told me everything?"

Soon they'd be heading into morning, but she had no more intention of pointing that out to him than she wanted those specifics. By now all the Brahmas were down and sleeping. A couple were snoring. Her shoulder had gone numb from the weight of his arm, and his flesh must be sore from her constant rubbing. "You know it all," he muttered. "Every dirty secret."

"It isn't dirty. It's been your reality all your life."

"Maybe. How do *you* feel?"

"I'm trying to—" A yawn stopped her. She stifled it, but the second one came without warning. She couldn't feel her legs. Although the day had been hot, she'd started to shiver. "Kade, I can't think," she admitted.

* * * * *

The rodeo organizers had given him the key to a groundskeeper's place. It consisted of a small kitchen-living room and even smaller bedroom barely large enough for the double bed crammed into it. Still, Kade had determined that it was better suited for two people than her trailer. Although he'd been punch-drunk with the need to sleep himself, he'd all but carried Maita to it. He hadn't known whether she'd agree to come in. When she did, he told himself at least she hadn't been disgusted by his revelations.

Of course she might have been too tired to fully comprehend.

After using the bathroom, she slumped onto the bed and started to remove her boots. He finished the job then thanked her when she did the same for him. They both acted half-drunk as they stripped off the rest of their clothes. He'd pulled back the thin coverlet and shown her that at least the sheets were clean.

"Wonderful," she'd said on the tail of another yawn. "Better than sleeping standing up, which I think I could do tonight."

They lay down facing each other, legs intertwined, her snuggled against him. He remembered starting to stroke the small of her back then nothing.

Now he was awake. Lying in the darkness, he couldn't tell how much time had passed or what had interrupted his sleep. Beside him, she slept soundlessly.

Why? Why did I tell her what I did, dump everything?

Don't you know? some alter personality demanded. *You dumb shit, you've fallen in love.*

Rocked to the core he started to sit up. His exhausted body refused to comply so he settled back into the mattress and lightly ran his hand over Maita's spine down to the swell of her buttocks. He knew the feel, the texture, of her flesh. Well, why wouldn't he? She'd been his, completely.

His mind seemed to skip a beat, then splinter. Thoughts piled one upon the other. Countless women flitted into view only to evaporate. They were tall and short, thin, muscular, heavy-set. All were naked. All wore restraints he was responsible for.

This was his life, woman after woman after woman. Endless delights. Control and power. Breasts and clits, thighs and bellies — all for him.

Until they left.

Until he left them.

* * * * *

"Kade? Kade, it's morning."

Technically dawn had just begun to break, but Maita knew he would soon have to go to work. She felt hungover from lack of sleep, and memories of what he'd told her last night had only begun to seep through the mental fog.

When he continued to lay there with his eyes closed, she crawled out of bed and used the bathroom. Maybe she shouldn't feel self-conscious about being naked, but thinking he might need back his space and privacy after everything he'd revealed, she reached for her clothes on the floor.

"Are you leaving?" he asked.

"I need a shower and clean clothes."

"And once you're ready for the day, what then?"

His eyes said the question wasn't a casual one, but she didn't have an answer for him. After a moment, he got up and went into the bathroom to urinate. By the time he rejoined her in the miniscule room, she'd put on her blouse over her naked breasts.

"You can't handle it?" he asked. He seemed unconcerned with his nudity. "Learning my mother's friends taught me how to use pain to enhance climaxes is more than you needed to know."

"I didn't say that."

"You don't have to. I see it in your eyes."

"Don't try to do my thinking for me, Kade. We're both operating on only a few hours of sleep. Let's get this rodeo over with and then—"

"We have time for sex."

"What is this, a proposition?" she snapped. She hated the way she sounded but couldn't help herself. Fully awake now, she could no longer hide from the thought that had tried to intrude last night. The conditions she couldn't live with and remain part of his world. "Have you ever courted a woman?" she asked. Damn it, she sounded like a shrew. "You know, flowers and candy."

"What is this about?"

Having a heated conversation and trying not to touch in a room that wouldn't make a decent prison cell was getting on her nerves. Damn him for waking up with an erection. Damn her for getting turned on from looking at him.

"About?" she repeated. *Kade, I've never felt like this before, never thought I'd fall in love, never been so vulnerable.* "Nothing that's happened between us has gone according to the books. We've never had a normal date. We haven't gone out for dinner, a movie, a drive." Thank goodness she'd picked up her jeans. Otherwise she wouldn't know what to do with her hands. As for him, he was running his hands over his thighs.

"I guess I don't know how to do those things."

Neither did she.

"Go," he said when she remained silent. "Give yourself the space you need."

She glanced at the door but didn't move toward it. "What are you going to do?"

"What I know how to."

"Here? Today?" She felt sick.

"Not that. I have a rodeo to pull off."

"Oh," she whispered.

"You thought—"

"How was I to know? I don't have your schedule."

"I told you, I don't mix the two."

"You're right, you did. I guess I forgot."

He reached her in less than two steps, but all he did was cup his hand under her chin, lift her face, and kiss her, briefly.

"I'm sorry," he said. "I should have known telling you would be too much. But I couldn't go on lying."

He hadn't lied. Until last night he'd omitted. "Whatever you want to call it, you got it behind you. Laid everything on the table. I-I appreciate it."

His hands dropped to his side. Except for his cock, he sagged. "But you couldn't handle it."

"Of course I can!" she snapped. "I'm no hothouse flower, no innocent. I'm not appalled because you lost your virginity to your mother's best friend while your mother monitored the activity."

He looked surprised that she'd repeated what had taken him a long time to tell her. "Then what's wrong?"

Everything. Nothing. I don't know.

If she walked out that door, something would have broken between them. True, she could return once she'd pulled herself together, or he might seek her out later. But he'd placed something precious in her hands via his revelation. Either she acknowledged the gift, now, or he'd spend the rest of his life believing he'd been wrong to trust her.

"I've changed my mind," she told him and slipped off her blouse. "I want sex after all. I want to fuck—you." *Not think. Not issue ultimatums. Just fuck.*

"Why?"

"Isn't that obvious? I'm horny."

"And I'm handy?"

"What is this about?" she demanded. It occurred to her that he hadn't taken his attention off her eyes. She might as well have been wrapped in layers of clothing for all he cared.

"I don't know." His shrug reached all the way to his ready-for-action cock. "Something hasn't been said here."

He was right, damn him. But she could only take this one step at a time. "I'm offering." She cupped her breasts for emphasis. "Are you accepting?"

"If I do, will you tell me what you're thinking?"

How well the man knew her, maybe better than she knew herself. "I want to," she admitted. "But I'm not quite ready." *And having sex, at this moment, might be the only way I'll know whether I can take the risk.*

"I see," he muttered although obviously he didn't.

Instead of touching her, he continued to study her, slowly, as if savoring each inch of the journey. His eyes stroked her skin and heated her. Although she managed not to move toward him, she couldn't keep her hands on her breasts still. She massaged them until her nipples hardened then lightly fingered the sensitive nubs. Her mouth didn't want to stay closed. She felt feverish. She couldn't make the distinction between labia and clit, and cunt juice lubricated her inner passage. It took so little for him to ready her for intercourse, nothing more than a hot gaze and memories of what he'd done to her. This man restrained. He controlled. He forced. And she responded— boy, did she!

Suddenly her belly knotted. Blinking, she realized he'd stepped toward her. She took a backward step but stopped when the back of her knees connected with the bed. Another step, this time with his hands on his cock. In her mind, the organ became a dildo. He'd run it into her, power it up, and keep after her until she surrendered everything to his assault.

Although in a small way she knew her imagination was getting the best of her, she didn't try to free herself from the fantasy. Instead, she tried to put even more distance between them but only managed to lose her balance. She fell back, ass on the bed, arms behind her for support, legs apart.

"I thought you wanted this," he said with the distance between them down to inches.

"I do."

"Then what—"

"I don't know, all right!"

He nodded. Then he gripped her waist and slid her to the middle of the bed so only her feet dangled over the edge. When he joined her, his weight on the mattress pulled her toward him. She tried to turn away but stopped when he slid a hand between her legs. His fingers searched, coming ever closer to her opening. Thinking to even the playing field, she reached out, but although she briefly captured his penis, he pushed against her breasts and knocked her onto her back.

With no thought to trying to get him to leave her pussy alone, she renewed her efforts to lay claim to his cock. When he made no effort to deny her, she easily closed her fingers over the hard, hot organ. At the same moment, his index finger found her opening. With practiced patience, he turned his attention to exploring her wet cave.

Stay with the program, damn it, she admonished herself. But how could she even think to rule him if she couldn't keep her mind on anything except being stimulated. Her free hand gripped the tangled spread, and she arched her back, giving him access to her breasts if he wanted. Instead, he stroked and pushed, tickled and retreated. Of their own will, her hips moved without rhythm. She lifted her pelvis in invitation. He acknowledged by increasing his penetration to two fingers.

"Fast. So fast!" she gasped.

"Too fast," he muttered. Still, he continued to work her, and she didn't try to still her hips. She again struggled to concentrate on what she could do to his cock, but all her fingers wanted to do was hold him.

"More!" she insisted when he touched her clit. "Please, more!"

"If I do, you'll explode. It's too soon."

Oh. She was still trying to judge his wisdom when he abruptly pulled out of her, gripped her hips, and flipped her onto her belly which forced her to release his penis. Uneasy and excited at the same time, she turned her head so she could study him. He knelt beside her, leaned low over her, and raked his teeth over her buttocks. The sensation came close to lifting her off the bed. If he bit—

Her toes and fingers curled inward the instant he ran his damp tongue over the spot where his teeth had just been. He continued to bathe her. Each wet stroke reached beyond her skin and found a connection with her pussy. Moaning, she turned away so, maybe, he wouldn't see the naked lust she knew lay in her eyes.

She wished she could give him equal pleasure, but those thoughts only flitted through her because inch by wonderful inch his tongue and teeth forged a path. When he reached the base of her spine, he spread her butt cheeks and feathered his tongue along the valley, stopping short of her ass. She shuddered, her muscles continued their disjointed dance.

He continued working her buttocks, hips, the insides of her thighs with his mouth. Her mons pressed against the spread, and her pussy felt trapped, but she vowed to remain accessible to him for as long as he wanted.

Or so she believed until he moved between her legs, pushing her onto her knees with her legs spread wide at the same time. She didn't try to lift her upper body. Instead, she gasped and shuddered and hung at the edge of climax while he bathed her labia. Soon, soon, he'd conquer her most sensitive organ, but although she thought she was prepared, when he closed his lips around her clit, she nearly came undone.

She couldn't — couldn't stop him!

But even as she frantically worked herself onto her back again, she acknowledged something incredible. He wasn't bending her to his will. Whatever she wanted to do this morning would happen.

Delighted with her newfound knowledge, she spread her legs so he was again housed between them. Reaching up, she gripped his shoulders and leveraged herself off the spread. They touched from pelvis to breasts. He leaned away slightly to support her weight and slid his hands behind her buttocks. The position, although not entirely comfortable, sustained her while she studied him.

He needed a shave. His hair looked as if it had never seen a comb. A sleep-crease marked his cheek.

"What do you see?" he asked.

"A man. One who accepts what life made him and apologizes for nothing."

"How do you feel about that?"

"Your background is what it is, like mine."

"Good." His mouth moved as if he was about to say something. Then he touched his lips to hers and she returned the gesture and nothing else mattered. At first his lips barely grazed hers, like a boy testing the waters with some girl he has a crush on. But she was no shy young girl. She matched his pace and slowly, wonderfully, the contact increased. Their mouths parted, tongues came out, and the dance heated. She allowed him entrance and then asked for and received the same gift.

For a moment she thought he was leaning toward her. Too late she realized he was no longer trying to maintain them in an upright position and fell back on the bed. He stretched over her, arms on either side of her shoulders, legs out behind him and his knees supporting his lower body.

"Got you," he announced.

Earlier in their relationship, the announcement would signal a final rope tie or a chain lock slipping into place, but this time he held her with his greater size, his warmth and muscle. Her trust of him.

Signaling acceptance, she remained still under him, arms out, legs spread so he'd fit. His cock brushed her labia, and with his every breath, it slid over her hot and willing flesh.

"You're ready?" he asked.

"Yes. Yes!"

While she tried to keep him in focus, he rocked back. Although the need to house him in her throbbed through her, she simply lifted her hips. Flesh slid over flesh. As the contact deepened, she again took hold of his shoulders. He began pumping into her. His expression turned intense, a man concentrating on one thing. He filled her, his shaft adding more fuel until she forgot everything except this moment, this man. Her cunt muscles began to spasm, holding him prisoner and bringing her closer to her personal mountain.

His thrusts became long, slow, and powerful. With each drive, she felt herself sliding a few inches on the bed. The friction along her back contrasted with their sweat-slickened bellies. Discomfort warred with pleasure, the sensations locking her even tighter into herself.

Thinking to give him something to ram himself against, she dug her heels into the sheet, but although their movement slowed, it didn't stop. Her head was over the side of the bed before she realized she'd reached the edge.

He stopped, cock buried deep and full. She lifted her head and stared at him. A smile touched his beautiful mouth. "Trust me," he said and used his thighs and cock to shove her even further. For a moment she hung in space. Her grip shifted to his waist, he reached out and placed his hands on the floor.

"Trust you?" she chided. "Are you crazy?"

"Probably."

Their gymnastics had caused him to slip out of her, but he quickly remedied that and again began pumping. Because the alternative was to bang the back of her head on the floor, she gripped his waist, dug her heels into the bed and absorbed him. The change of position brought his cock fully against the front of her pussy.

No longer slow and long, he drove into her over and over again. Trying to brace herself became impossible so she rode with him. They now moved as one. Her pussy tightened down around him, held him long and strong. Her cunt muscles burned, adding to the fast-building climax.

When it hit, she dug her nails into his flesh, pulled herself up so her breasts kissed his chest. A sharp cry exploded from her. Another followed. Then her contractions came one upon another, signaling her climax's breadth and intensity.

Love you, love you, love you.

* * * * *

"Enough?"

"God yes."

"Think you're going to be able to ride tonight?"

"Think you can run your end of the show?"

Kade didn't answer, not that she cared. Once she'd regained control over her body, she'd taken note of the well-used carpet and had crawled back on the bed. Kade had joined her and she now lay in the crook of his arm, his deflated penis and her spent cunt all but forgotten. Thoughts and emotions she'd shoved aside earlier came back to life, but she held them at bay and concentrated on him.

"Your trailer doesn't have a shower in it, does it?" he asked. "This one isn't much, but it'll work."

"I appreciate it." She made no effort to get up. Their sex had quite literally blown her away with its intensity, her body felt satiated. And yet—

"Are you ovulating?"

"What? I-I don't think so. We forgot again."

When he didn't respond, she wondered if maybe he hadn't forgotten protection. She started to sit up. He tightened his hold. "Not yet. We have things to talk about."

Yes, we do. "Like what?"

"Maita, I know you raised yourself. After what was done to you, you don't want anyone telling you how to live your life."

"I hear a *but*," she prompted when he fell silent.

"Yeah, you do." He ran a hand along her neck then started a slow journey toward her breasts. "Damn it, you're living out of a trailer. You don't know where your next paycheck is coming from. If you get hurt, how are you going to support yourself?"

"I have insurance. Besides, it's my problem, not yours." In truth she'd been asking herself the same things.

"It won't be if you're carrying my child."

My child. Touched by the emotion behind his words, she watched as he began playing with her nipple. Much more of that and she'd want a repeat performance of what had taken place half on the bed and half on the floor. "Women have been known to raise children alone. Your mother did it."

"Hell of a job she did! Almost as good as the one that was done to you. Besides, it doesn't have to be like that for you, for us."

Sudden fear gripped her, prompting her to pull out of his embrace and stand. Being naked made her feel so damn vulnerable. Or was her nudity responsible?

"What is this, a proposal?" The moment she asked, she regretted uttering the words.

He sat up. "You don't look like a woman who's just been proposed to. In truth, you look as if you just got thrown and stomped on."

"Do I?"

He nodded and stood but made no move to touch her. "What was what we just did?" he demanded. "A roll in the hay? You needed an itch scratched and I was handy?"

"Stop it!" She fought the impulse to run. "Our relationship has never been like that."

"What has it been?"

Has? Past tense? She felt lightheaded and on the brink of tears. "Life-changing," she whispered.

His nod made her wonder if he felt the same way. But he dealt in numbers, boobs, butts. Women were a dime a dozen to him. "Did you try to make me pregnant?"

He groaned. "I don't know."

"What?"

"What do you want me to say?" He started to reach for her then stopped. His gaze slipped from her eyes down over her body. "Maita, when that bronc threw you and I carried you out of the arena...I don't think I've ever felt such fear."

"I...was all right."

"I know. And I've seen countless cowboys thrown. Few are badly injured. Always before I figured they knew what they were getting into. Their risks weren't my business."

He was staring at her feet now, but she doubted he saw them. "But when I held you, something changed."

"What did?"

"I don't know. Damn it! I have to stop saying that! You changed something about me," he said and met her eyes again.

"I understand," she admitted. If only she dared touch him! "I felt— I felt as if I'd shifted inside. The world didn't look the same anymore, my priorities changed."

"Because I fucked you in ways you've never been fucked." He sounded bitter.

"No." She shook her head. "Yes, that was part of it but not all."

"You mean it?"

This man had always been in control. No matter whether he was handling stock or women, he knew what he was doing. Didn't he? "When I first realized what you did, I was both scared and eager to have you do me. At the same time I was seeing another part of you. Kade, in many respects we live in the same world."

"What respects?"

"Rodeos. Man against animal. Challenge and risk. A return to a time when things were basic."

"No safety nets. Life and death played out daily."

"Exactly." She took his hands. A moment later she slid into his arms. But even as she lifted her head for another kiss, she trembled.

"What is it?" he asked when they were done. "Something's still wrong."

If she was as brave as rodeo fans thought she was, she would walk away from him and be done with whatever had gone on between them. But she couldn't, not yet. "I can't do it, Kade."

"Can't do what?"

"Share you with those other women." The words exhausted her. Although she'd spoken the death notes to their relationship, she continued to cling to him. "You want me to give up riding, but what about what you're asking me to do?"

He stepped back but continued to hold her. She felt small and weak in his grip and wondered when she'd die inside.

"I'm sorry," he whispered.

She waited for the rest. If she could bring herself to speak, she'd tell him she understood—he couldn't change who he was any more than she could. They'd shake hands and go their own way. She'd continue to ride. He'd return to his ranch with the private building. And if she turned out to be pregnant—

"Sorry I didn't tell you this before," he said. "I've worked with my last woman."

Mute, she stared up at him.

"Maita, you don't know how much I wanted to tell you of my decision, but I needed to know how you felt about me before I did."

"You were afraid of being vulnerable."

He seemed surprised by her wisdom, but it wasn't that at all. What she understood was vulnerability, nothing else.

Before she could begin to pull her thoughts together, someone knocked on the door. "We've got a problem, boss," a man yelled.

Kade swore under his breath. But instead of reaching for his clothes, he drew her against him. His erection grew. "Tonight," he said.

"Tonight. Kade?"

"What?"

"I love you."

"Oh god." His grip tightened. "I love you, too."

Epilogue

"I'm surrounded by women," Kade muttered. "Everywhere I look, more females."

"You're complaining?" Maita teased and repositioned herself in the saddle. "Isn't this every man's dream?" She indicated the half dozen barrel racers who were working their horses in the corral she'd had him build on his property — their property now.

"If they were falling all over themselves trying to get to me, maybe." He pasted on a stern expression she might have believed if he didn't have his hand on her thigh. "But all they care about is their damn horses."

"Speaking of, I've got to get to work."

"Says who? This women's lib thing has gotten out of control. Aren't dutiful wives supposed to hop to when their husbands want a little midday quickie?" Despite the layer of denim between them, his sensual stroke accomplished what he obviously intended. Because she was on horseback with her mare between Kade and the other cowgirls she'd invited out to the ranch, hopefully they didn't know what was happening.

"Quickie?" She glared down at him. "No wonder I'm tired. You kept me busy most of the night."

"Busy?" His hand moved to her inner thigh, and he slid his fingers between her flesh and the saddle. "That's not what I'd call it. If I recall, you were the insatiable one."

"Me? What about you?"

Laughing, Kade stood on tiptoe. She leaned over and kissed her groom full and rich. *Groom?* Technically they'd gotten past the newlywed stage since they'd been married for three weeks now, but the honeymoon which had begun the last night of the Pendleton rodeo showed no sign of waning. If not for the strain on her back and her desire to work with the cowgirls she'd been competing against, she could have gone on kissing him, and more.

"All right, here's the deal," Kade said. His hand remained on her. "Since the vet's coming in about a half hour, I'll relent and let my woman go do her thing. But she's going to have to pay me back for depriving me of my husbandly rights."

"What did you have in mind?"

This time he laughed loud enough to startle her usually placid mare. "It's for me to know and you to find out. Don't forget, your man has a lot of tricks up his sleeve. A few tools and an occasional rope."

Did he ever! If the others knew she and Kade had spent last night playing their own version of tag, they might kick her out of the informal barrel racing practice sessions—either that or insist on participating.

Fat chance. What went on in the bedroom and anywhere else they could think of was for the two of them.

Kade swatted her mare on the rump and turned away, but instead of joining the others, she continued to study the man she loved beyond comprehension. The last night at Pendleton had been a time for many things. Of course the sex had nearly blown the top off her head, but she'd also learned of a man who'd long wanted to belong with one woman but hadn't known it until the right one had entered his life. She'd had revelations of her own, admissions of a lonely existence and a need to be part of someone she trusted. Although she'd always love competing, he'd changed her priorities. Now he came first — and second.

"Give it a rest!" one of the cowgirls called out. "You can scratch his itch later. We've got work to do."

"I'm coming." She urged her mare toward the women she already considered friends. They might compete against each other during a rodeo, but they helped her hone her skills in the rodeo event she and Kade had compromised on, and she did the same for them.

Compromise was good. It meant she could continue to challenge herself doing something she loved. At the same time, Kade no longer endured the bareback event wondering whether he'd have to rush his wife and the mother of his future children to the emergency room.

"We're taking bets," the woman who'd yelled at her said when she joined them. "I say you're already pregnant. Carol says three months before you're knocked up even if you're taking every birth control product on the market. Jane here doesn't give a damn. She just wishes she was getting half the sex you obviously are. So...which of us wins?"

"Not until next year at the earliest," she told them. "Before I give this all up for motherhood —" She indicated the waiting barrels. "I'm going to the finals."

"Does your stud agree?"

"He does now."

"Meaning?"

"Compromise." And the world's most understanding husband.

About the author:

Vonna welcomes mail from readers. You can write to her c/o Ellora's Cave Publishing at 1056 Home Avenue, Akron, OH 44310-3502.

Why an electronic book?

We live in the Information Age—an exciting time in the history of human civilization in which technology rules supreme and continues to progress in leaps and bounds every minute of every hour of every day. For a multitude of reasons, more and more avid literary fans are opting to purchase e-books instead of paperbacks. The question to those not yet initiated to the world of electronic reading is simply: *why?*

1. *Price.* An electronic title at Ellora's Cave Publishing and Cerridwen Press runs anywhere from 40-75% less than the cover price of the <u>exact same title</u> in paperback format. Why? Cold mathematics. It is less expensive to publish an e-book than it is to publish a paperback, so the savings are passed along to the consumer.

2. *Space.* Running out of room to house your paperback books? That is one worry you will never have with electronic novels. For a low one-time cost, you can purchase a handheld computer designed specifically for e-reading purposes. Many e-readers are larger than the average handheld, giving you plenty of screen room. Better yet, hundreds of titles can be stored within your new library—a single microchip. (Please note that Ellora's Cave and Cerridwen Press does not endorse any specific brands. You can check our website at www.ellorascave.com or

www.cerridwenpress.com for customer recommendations we make available to new consumers.)

3. *Mobility.* Because your new library now consists of only a microchip, your entire cache of books can be taken with you wherever you go.

4. *Personal preferences are accounted for.* Are the words you are currently reading too small? Too large? Too...**ANNOYING**? Paperback books cannot be modified according to personal preferences, but e-books can.

5. *Instant gratification.* Is it the middle of the night and all the bookstores are closed? Are you tired of waiting days—sometimes weeks—for online and offline bookstores to ship the novels you bought? Ellora's Cave Publishing sells instantaneous downloads 24 hours a day, 7 days a week, 365 days a year. Our e-book delivery system is 100% automated, meaning your order is filled as soon as you pay for it.

Those are a few of the top reasons why electronic novels are displacing paperbacks for many an avid reader. As always, Ellora's Cave and Cerridwen Press welcomes your questions and comments. We invite you to email us at service@ellorascave.com, service@cerridwenpress.com or write to us directly at: 1056 Home Ave. Akron OH 44310-3502.

NEED A MORE EXCITING WAY TO PLAN YOUR DAY?

ELLORA'S
CAVEMEN
2006 CALENDAR

COMING THIS FALL

THE
ELLORA'S CAVE
LIBRARY

Stay up to date with Ellora's Cave Titles
in Print with our Quarterly Catalog.

COMING TO A BOOKSTORE NEAR YOU!

ELLORA'S CAVE
2005
BEST SELLING AUTHORS TOUR

Discover for yourself why readers can't get enough of the multiple award-winning publisher Ellora's Cave. Whether you prefer e-books or paperbacks, be sure to visit EC on the web at www.ellorascave.com for an erotic reading experience that will leave you breathless.

www.ellorascave.com

Printed in the United States
36524LVS00001B/145-147